The Strongest Whiskee

B. Love

Prolific Pen Pusher

Prologue

A volcano of giggles erupted from Whiskee's belly. She was spending the evening with her best friend, which was one of her favorite things to do. Mahogany was Whiskee's favorite person, and she didn't think that would ever change. As often was the case, what they were laughing at didn't warrant the extreme mirth, but when they started laughing it was hard for them to stop.

Mahogany clutched Whiskee's arm as she begged,

"Girl, *please*, stop. If you snort one more time, I'm going to pee on myself."

"Then stop talking about that man! I can't take another second of it."

"It's not my fault! I swear to God when he took his boxers off it smelled like bologna."

"So what excuse did you give to leave?" Whiskee asked, wiping a tear that had fallen.

"Excuse? I didn't give him one. He knew what was up. I don't even know why he played with my time like that. As soon I smelled it, I gagged. I got the hell up out of there expeditiously!"

"That's what you get for thinking because he was fine the sex would be good. I bet you won't go to a hotel with a stranger from the bar again."

Another surge of laughter escaped the pair.

"I learned my lesson for sure. I could have handled a small lil thang thang, but a stinky one? Nuh unh!"

"Mahogany, shut *up*!"

As Whiskee rolled onto her side, her brother, Carlos, charged into her room. Her first instinct was to yell at him for not only invading her private time with Mahogany, but for doing so without knocking. However, the distraught look on his face caused her to sit up.

"What's wrong, Los?"

"It's Pops. He collapsed at the meeting. We need to go to the hospital now!"

Ghosts of their laughter followed them out of the room as Whiskee and Mahogany hurried behind Carlos. For every question Whiskee asked, Carlos had no answer.

"Why weren't you at the meeting with him?" Whiskee asked. "Now he's heading to the hospital alone."

"We'll be there soon," Mahogany assured her, grabbing her hand and giving it a gentle squeeze.

"He gon' be aight, Whis. It was probably just..." Carlos's head shook as he tried to comfort his sister, but his disbelief of his own assurance was shining through.

Silence found them as they hopped into Carlos's Maybach truck. Whiskee whispered silent prayers as they headed toward the hospital.

Those prayers were seemingly unanswered.

By the time they arrived, Robert had died from a heart attack.

No amount of comfort from her brother or best friend soothed Whiskee. She'd already lost her mother years ago because of a murderous robber who'd killed Renee in front of her. Now, she didn't have a father either. Twenty-nine years old seemed too old to feel like an orphan, but that was exactly how Whiskee felt as she cursed God for taking the only parent she had left.

Whiskee

S
ix Months Later

GRIEF WAS AN ERRATIC THING. SOMETIMES, IT WAS A
gentle bite. Sometimes, it swallowed you whole. Today,
grief swallowed me whole. Years ago, I didn't think *any* pain
could top the night my mother was murdered, but losing my
father six months ago did. His loss was harder because he
was the last parent I had. Plus, I was a daddy's girl. I was in
awe of him.

I'd never called him Daddy, always his full name. When
I learned it, it rolled off my tongue sweetly and made him
smile every time I said it—even as an adult. My father,
Robert Carter, spoiled me. He shielded me and took care of
me. Robert Carter made sure there was nothing in this
world that I wanted but couldn't have.

Outside of material things, my father spoiled me with
his love, time, and attention too. Even with his loyalty to the
streets, he made sure I never doubted that I was his priority.

A part of me believed he stayed close to me because we'd lost my mom. Though I never asked it of him, he went above and beyond to fill her void. Truth was, he never would have been able to. There was nothing or no one who could have taken the place of my mother's love. And now, there was nothing or no one who could take the place of my father's love.

That truth had me curling up a little tighter in the center of my bed. I didn't do too much these days. Very rarely did I leave the house. Actually, I could count on one hand how many times I did. Anything I needed, I had delivered, or Carlos or Mahogany brought it to me. Mahogany had been instrumental in helping me keep my sanity. Sisterhood was a form of therapy, and in my best friend, my heart found peace and relief.

There was no job that required my presence. Even with me having my cosmetology license, I didn't use it in a salon. Doing hair and makeup was a passion for me, but my father took such great care of me that I'd never had to work a real job a day in my life. I did hair and makeup for close friends when they had special occasions, but even that had been halted since my daddy had been taken from me.

There was no man or child that required my attention. Robert Carter hadn't felt like any of the men I dated were worthy of me. I stayed with him and my brother in our seven-bedroom mansion and had no plans to leave anytime soon. Now, I didn't know what I was going to do. It was hard staying in this home with so many memories of my father... but I also loved feeling closer to him—being able to go in his room to touch his clothes or smell his cologne.

A fucking heart attack.

A fucking heart attack took my father away from me.

Just the thought had my eyes closing as they watered. I

inhaled a deep, shaky breath, gripping the necklaces around my neck. One was a heart filled with petals of the lilacs we had at his funeral. The other was filled with his ashes.

Robert Carter loved lilacs because they were Mama's favorite. He would get them for her all the time. After she died, he still got them and kept them in the kitchen, since that was where she spent the bulk of her time throughout the day because she loved to cook.

There hadn't been any purple lilacs in the kitchen in six months.

It was cold, dark, and ugly now.

Light tapping on my bedroom door was followed up with, "Whis, can I come in?"

I wanted to tell Carlos no, but it wasn't fair of me to keep pushing him away. He'd lost both parents too. This was a time for us to cling to each other and help each other heal. All I wanted to do was lay in bed and sleep. I was in denial about the depression I'd been in. Or maybe it wasn't depression. Maybe it was just... an overwhelming inability to mentally and emotionally escape the sadness that consumed me. Either way, I didn't want to be around anyone, but I told Carlos that he could come in anyway.

Carlos wasted no time walking through my room and opening the blinds to my windows. My eyes squinted as I sat up in bed.

"What are you doing?" I asked, though it was clear.

"Getting some light in here. All you've been doing is laying in here in darkness. It's time to snap out of it, sis."

My eyes rolled as I lifted my knees to my chest. I didn't bother arguing with him. Carlos, like our father, was a determined man and he *always* did what he wanted.

"I'm just going to close them when you leave," I grumbled, making him smile.

7

He sat on the edge of my bed. He looked so much like *him*. Gritting my teeth, I tried to look away to avoid the younger version of my father, but I was unable to. Looking at my brother was the closest thing I'd have to looking at Robert Carter. I had to take full advantage of that.

"I don't doubt that, but you'll be leavin' soon too."

My lip poked out slightly and brows wrinkled as my head tilted in confusion. "I don't have any plans."

"I made plans for us."

Rolling my eyes, I crossed my arms over my chest. "What plans, Carlos?"

"I need a solid from you, Whiskee, and I need you to hear me out fully before you say yes or no." Just him saying that had me wanting to say no, but I remained silent and nodded so he could continue. "I made dinner plans tonight for us and Tim Smith. I'm sure his son and nephew will probably be there, too, but I'on really give a fuck about them."

"Tim Smith?" I repeated. The name was familiar, but I wasn't sure why. It had to be someone my father did business with. "Who is that?"

"That was Pops' supplier. Tim is big on keeping things in the family. Pops was the only man Tim supplied that wasn't working directly under him or his family."

"Okay?" I replied skeptically, not sure what this meant or why it had anything to do with me. "Are we almost out of money or something? Where are you going with this?"

"We're not out of money," he said quickly, running his hand over his face—a gesture our father did when he was stressed. God. They looked so much alike. Same caramel-brown skin, low-cut wavy hair, and dark eyes. "But I need to keep the organization up and running. This street shit is all I know. I can't switch suppliers right now. Our customers are used to the product we get from Tim. I also can't establish a new relationship with someone who will expect me to pay more for the product. Pops had built a great rapport with Tim. Plus, his reach is large, so he was able to buy more than anyone working for Tim. Because of that, he gave Pops a good discount."

"I get all that. So you want to go to the dinner to make sure you can continue to work with him?"

"Yeah."

"Why do I have to be there?"

"Like I said, family is important. I know I'll have a better chance of convincing him to work with me if we show up as a united front."

I felt like Carlos was leaving something out. If family was so important to Tim, I would have thought our father would have brought me around sooner. If he didn't, it was for a reason. Robert Carter didn't play about me. I was hidden from his street life for my safety. My father was very proud of his children, and Carlos's ability to operate and stand by his side. Being a part of that lifestyle had never been a desire of mine. I benefited from it because of the riches and power that came with it, but sitting in on meetings and being around our father's supplier seemed... unnatural.

"It's just us now," Carlos continued. "I need you, Whis. I need to be able to continue to provide for us and maintain the lifestyle Pops got us used to. We need to stay in business, and for that to happen, I can't lose this connect."

Massaging my temples, I sighed. A dinner with a drug supplier was the last thing I wanted to do tonight, but I would. Carlos was right—we were all the other had. Our parents came to Memphis from Chicago after they were married. We didn't have any other family members here, and we weren't really close to the family we had in Chicago. When we were kids, our parents took us to Chicago to spend Christmas break with our family but that was it. Once we became adults those trips stopped. By then, our grandparents were gone, and that family time no longer felt the same.

"Okay, I'll go, but I don't want to stay long."

A grin spread Carlos's lips as he stood and walked over to give me a hug.

"I knew you wouldn't let me down." After sniffing me, he added, "Make sure you take a bath. You stink."

With a sniggle, I mushed him away by his forehead. "I do *not* stink. I took a shower last night, asshole."

"Well I can tell you didn't take one this morning. You smellin' a lil ripe, sis."

Even though I knew that wasn't true, it still made me laugh because of how he covered his nose.

"If I'm so stinky, get out of my room."

"Shit, say less. Be ready at six."

My eyes rolled as I released the last of my laughter and sat on the edge of my bed. After checking the time on my phone, I sighed. I had three hours to not only find something to wear and do my hair but do the maintenance I'd neglected for the last six months as well. I needed to shave and do my nails, and my brows were in dire need of a good threading. Hopefully, getting ready for dinner and putting a little pride in my appearance would help me start to feel better.

Whiskee

When I called Mahogany and told her Carlos and I were going out tonight, she was so excited she decided to come over and help me find something to wear. Since this was technically a business dinner, we decided on a Nadia satin gown from A.L.C. Its ochre-yellow hue looked phenomenal against my whisky-colored skin. I loved satin and silk because they accentuated my petite yet curvy frame. A frame I'd spent the last three years building to my desired taste.

I didn't chisel and tone my abs and waist and grow my ass for a man's approval. My body and style of dress had never been for the male gaze. It was for myself, and I loved dressing nice for the girls. There was nothing better to me than a woman hyping another woman up. I was truly a girl's girl. Men enjoying my looks and style was often an extra.

It didn't take long to find my outfit. The bulk of my time was spent on my maintenance. As it neared five p.m., I finished my pin curls and got ready to start on my makeup, which was the last thing I'd have to do.

"Okay, Whis. White or red?"

Turning in the seat of my vanity, I smiled as Mahogany held up two bottles of wine by the mini bar in the sitting area of my room.

"Hmm... let's keep it light and go with Moscato."

"Gotcha."

As she poured us both a glass, I turned and looked at my reflection in the mirror. The lack of eating had sunken my cheeks. My eyes were dark and puffy from crying daily. I was almost ashamed of how I'd temporarily let myself go, but I chose instead to give myself grace. With a loss like the one I'd endured, I didn't think anyone would blame me for not giving a damn about how I looked.

"Are you nervous?" she asked, handing me the wine. I took a sip then set it on the vanity.

"A little. It feels like I'm being included in a boys' club that I've never wanted any parts of." Chuckling, I selected my foundation for the evening. "I've never wanted to be included in the business and Daddy kept me out of it. I hope Los doesn't think that's about to change."

"Did you tell him that when he asked you to come?"

I shook my head. "No, but I will. I want to make sure he understands this is just a one-time thing."

"I don't blame you. The less you know about that life-style the better. I know it's what he and your father have done for years, but still. Mama Renee stayed out of it, and I want you to stay out of it too."

I completely agreed with her about that. I think Mama's chosen delusion about what Daddy did was what allowed her to live with such peace. To her, he wasn't a drug dealer; he was simply a provider. She didn't ask questions about the business... nor did she ask questions when he'd have to leave abruptly or come back home with busted knuckles and someone else's blood on his clothes. That ignorance kept her soft too.

We continued to talk as I did my makeup. Mahogany was an influencer and brand ambassador for several companies. I always did her hair and makeup when she had to do paid content. As we finished going over her schedule for the rest of the month, Carlos came in to see if I was ready. I told him I'd be down after slipping into my dress and shoes. The look he gave Mahogany didn't go unnoticed. She was looking great tonight herself in jean shorts, a button-down shirt, and cowboy boots.

This March weather was all over the place. One day it was warm enough for shorts and mini dresses and the next we'd need our coats. She was taking full advantage of the high sixty-degree weather today, though, and I didn't blame her.

Once I was ready to go, we headed out of my room hand-in-hand. I gave her a hug and kiss before she headed to her car, then I went toward Carlos's Maybach. Since he was outside on a phone call, he opened the door for me. He gave me a quick kiss on the cheek and said, "Lil stinky, you cleaned up nice."

"Shut up, boy, and let's go," I ordered through my laugh as I got in the car.

I could admit there were days where I didn't bother to get out of the bed for anything—not even to eat or shower—but that hadn't been the case yesterday or today, and that was progress.

He stayed outside for a while before getting in the truck, releasing a frustrated huff.

"What's wrong?" I asked as he started the truck.

"This nigga said he doesn't think we can do business together because he's heard I can be vitriol. I don't even know what the *fuck* that means."

His clipped tone and frown made it clear he was upset, but that didn't make it easy for me to hold my laugh in. Carlos was as hood as they come. Even with our parents providing for us as well as they did financially, he stayed in the hood with Daddy. As much as Mama wanted us both to go to college, Carlos didn't even make it out of high school. In the tenth grade, he decided he wanted to be a drug dealer like Daddy. Out of respect for Mama, Robert Carter told him he couldn't sell until he finished school.

Carlos forced Daddy's hand and started selling under one of his competitors. Because of that, Daddy took him under his wing. He dropped out of high school three months into that school year and hadn't regretted it since.

"*Vitriol,* or being *vitriolic,* means cruel or bitter criticism that is often unnecessary in my opinion."

"Hmm." His head bobbed and he massaged his goatee as he drove out of our gated driveway. "Is that really a bad thing, though? I need these niggas to fear and respect me as their boss."

"Yeah, but do you have to be unnecessarily cruel to do that?"

Carlos looked over at me briefly, tightening his grip on the steering wheel. "Do you think I'm cruel?"

I huffed, thinking it over carefully. Carlos, like Daddy, was a hard ass, but he was a softy at heart too.

"I can't say how you are in the streets. With me, you have your moments but you're a softy too. I think there have been times where you've said things in a crass or insensitive way, but you weren't trying to intentionally hurt anyone's feelings."

14

"You do always call me an asshole."

"Well... that's true." We shared a soft laugh. "But you're a good guy too. I love you, even though you really can get on my nerves."

"Aww," he cooed, trying to pull me toward him by my neck.

"Carlos, stop!" I yelled with a smile as he kissed my cheek.

"I love you, Whis. For real," he confessed as he released me. "And I promise, everything I'm doing now is for you. For us. I told Pops if he got out of here too soon that I'd take care of you just like he did. Remember that tonight."

His statement, though sweet, made my heart drop. "I love you too, and I appreciate you. Will this meeting make me forget that?"

Carlos's mouth twisted to the side. His head shook. "Honestly... I don't know."

Beethoven

The Day Before

My time was a luxury, and I often made sure it wasn't wasted. Not too often was I able to link up with the crew, so tonight was special. It was me, Asylum, Merc, Bully, and Karrington. When we got together, we often shut the place down. Life had been progressing for my guys in ways I wasn't sure was possible for me.

Asylum, Merc, and Bully all had new babies and the loves of their lives at home. Karrington was single like me, but his heart was being held captive by Luna Ray—a married woman. A married woman who kept her distance from him because, in my opinion, she knew it was dangerous for the two of them to be around each other. I wouldn't say she didn't love her husband, but there was no doubt in my mind that my boy truly had her heart.

Before I could fully settle into my evening out, I got a

phone call from Pops. With our line of business, I couldn't ignore his calls. Standing, I excused myself and headed out of the lounge as I answered with, "Yeah?"

"Meet me at the steakhouse."

"Now?"

"Yeah."

Not waiting for me to agree, Pops ended the call. I should have known he was going to request my presence. The only time he called me was if something was wrong or we needed to meet. Other than that, we had our conversations face-to-face in the morning before we started making our moves or at the end of the day.

I went back inside the lounge and told my guys I'd have to get up with them later before heading to *At Steak*. It was one of several legal businesses we had and used to clean our money. Thankfully, it was in the downtown area not too far from the lounge. I ended up pulling up about seven minutes after the call.

The place was packed, which was no surprise to me. Patrons may have thought we had award-winning chefs in the kitchen, but nah. We employed men and women with felonies who could cook their asses off but not get a good-paying job anywhere else. The steakhouse was probably my favorite business of ours outside of the strip club because of the eclectic mix of people it brought in.

On any given day, you'd find a Grizzlies player in one booth, the mayor in another, and a drug dealer tucked in the back at his own table. As always, Pops was at his reserved table in the back by the exit. Seated with him was Terrance, his advisor; Denim, his money man; and my cousin, Omari —my right-hand man. The small group was alarming. Typically, our business meetings were planned and included most of our lieutenants so they could relay any necessary messages to their men.

I shook everyone's hand, then took the only other available seat at the table.

"Glad you could join us," Pops said, using his hand to dismiss the waitress, Amber, before she could ask us if we wanted to order any food.

"What is this about?" I asked.

"We have way too much product on the shelves." Pops leaned forward in his seat. "Robert being gone is causing us to take a huge loss. The product I'm not selling to him means millions that aren't coming in."

I hoped that wouldn't be the case. Robert had been gone for six months and Pops hadn't put anyone in his place yet. Robert was the only man outside of the family that Pops supplied in about a decade. At first, I wasn't sure if we could trust him. I didn't trust a man who had never been to jail or taken a life to do what we did, and both of those were the case when Pops first pulled Robert into the fold. Also, Pops was firm on keeping things in the family, and we weren't related to Robert.

I couldn't deny the reach Robert had. He went from bringing in five figures a month to six then seven. He was doing better than any of the other dealers, and losing him was truly a loss.

"Are you not willing to bring in another dealer?" Omari asked.

"Even if I did, they wouldn't have his reach, his reputation, and his customer base. It'll take me ten men to bring in the profit Robert was. For the last six months before he died, the man brought in seven figures a month. Now I can't speak on his profit after he paid his team, but that was the highest profit I had coming in from a dealer."

"What about his son?" I checked. "Is he going to continue to run the business? Did Robert have a plan in place for his death? Who's running that shit?"

"I set up a meeting with his son to discuss that. We're having dinner with him and his sister tomorrow. From what I've heard, Carlos wants to run the business, but I don't think that will work. He's young and not likable. Robert's men won't be loyal to him if he doesn't do a one-eighty. If I work with him, I feel like I'll end up killing him and taking over the organization myself, but I don't want to run it. I would give it to you."

And *that's* why he wanted to meet.

While I wouldn't deny I desired my own organization, I wasn't sure I wanted to get one that was taken from a father and son duo. Logically, I'd have to trust those men would be more dedicated to the money than their feelings about Robert and Carlos. On top of that, if I handled business differently from them, I ran the risk of losing money or men. It would have been my preference to build my team from the ground up, but I would be a damn fool to turn down an organization already in place with a multimillion-dollar clientele.

"I don't know about all that, but I do agree that we need to find a way to offset the loss in profit now that Robert is gone," I said, and we bounced ideas off each other for the next forty-five minutes.

Once the meeting was over, everyone began to leave. When it was just me, Pops, and Omari, my cousin asked, "What you gettin' into tonight?"

"We need to continue to talk," Pops answered for me. "You'll have to catch up with him later."

I could tell by Omari's hardened expression that he had something to say, but he bit his tongue. We shook hands and he excused himself from the table, leaving me and Pops alone. Finally, he called Amber over so we could order some food. I had no idea what else my father could possibly have to say...

Beethoven

It wasn't until we'd finished our steak and potatoes that Pops finally continued the conversation. I didn't know what else he could have wanted to say that required privacy, but I certainly wasn't expecting it to be, "I need you."

Out of my thirty-one years of life, my father had *never* uttered those words. In fact, I'd never heard him say he needed anyone. For as long as I could remember, he was always independent and the boss of all bosses. He didn't need anyone; people needed him—and that included my mother.

I didn't think they'd ever showed me a loving, healthy relationship. They showed me partnership and respect, but over the years, that faded away. My last year of high school, they divorced. Though my mother wanted me to live with her, I chose to stay with my father. We were closer, and as a man, I felt like it was more beneficial that I stay and continue to learn from him. While I wouldn't say I regretted that decision, not having my mother around to shield me from who my father truly was showed me sides of him I didn't respect.

When it came down to business, I admired Tim Smith, boss of all bosses. As a father and a man, I resented him. Even with that resentment, I understood that was my issue and cross to bear, not his. He gave all he could and raised me as best as he could. Where he lacked, it was my responsibility to ensure I became a better version of him.

My mother and I were closer than ever. I respected her for staying with him as long as she did, but I was glad she was free to live as she pleased and be loved in a healthy relationship. Though she hadn't remarried, she'd been in a committed relationship with the same man for the last five years. Pops was married to the streets. He was passionate about this shit and didn't let anything come before it, not even his family.

"What do you need?"

Sitting back in his seat, he took a sip of his Old Fashioned.

"Your uncles and cousins are concerned. You know they always felt some type of way when it came to Robert. Envy. They hated that I let a non-Smith into the fold. Worse, he did better than them."

I nodded my agreement. That had never been a secret. Even though Pops was the boss of all bosses, he ran his organization like it was any other business corporation. He had a second-in-command, stand-ins on the off chance anything happened to him, lieutenants who worked directly with our men, and an advisory board that operated to make sure my father did what was best for the business as a whole, not just himself. So he may have made the final decisions when it came to things, but if at any point they felt like he could no longer run things successfully, they could have him removed.

I hated that he put the board in place, even if it was three of my uncles. I didn't like that anyone could take what he'd worked so hard to build. But that board gave his men more peace to trust his lead, and with the way they put their lives and freedom on the line for us daily, I guess that was all that mattered.

"What they tryna do? Keep you from putting someone in his place?"

"They want someone in the family to take his product monthly. I made it clear to them that none of them are capable of handling such a large amount. If we don't start to move that weight, they gon' start to feel the effect of it."

"And it won't affect your plate for quite some time. So I'm not sure why they are against what you planned to do."

"It's not that they're fully against it; they just want me to do it their way. They want me to keep Carlos out and I can't agree with that."

"Aight, so what do you need me to do? Because I know if you don't fold, it'll be trouble with the lieutenants soon."

"Right. All it takes is for a few of them to question my authority and I'll have to go on a fuckin' killing spree." He sucked his teeth and sat up in his seat, crossing his arms on top of the table. "I don't have the time or desire to rebuild my leaders. That's where you come in."

I assumed he was going to say he wanted me to kill anyone who went against him and start anew. It wouldn't have been the first time I had blood on my hands after an order from my father, and I was sure it wouldn't be the last. I wasn't just his stand-in; I was his enforcer too. When I first started in the organization I was on the streets and in the field to learn the business. After about five years I was able

23

to advance and hadn't had to touch product to grow it or deal it since.

"You believe that keeping Carlos and Robert's team on is the best move financially?" I nodded. "And you agree that it'll be even better if we take over it completely?"

"I'on know about that, Pops." I sat up and looked around the restaurant, buying time while I tried to figure out how I wanted to say what I wanted to say. "It's not that I want to spare his life. I just feel like that's going to put a large weight on our shoulders. For the clientele Robert has, I'm not comfortable agreeing with taking over until after I've had time to see how his team moves and operates. If they can be trusted. If they will mesh with ours. The money would be good, but I need to know the risks will be worth it."

"I can respect that, and I also respect your honesty about it. That's why you're the only man I trust with this."

"With what, Pops? Just spit the shit out."

He chuckled and licked his lips. Usually he was straight to the point.

"The way to keep the peace with the board and still hold on to Robert's organization is to bring his son in with marriage since they aren't blood. That way, they will be family."

"I would agree, but you don't have a daughter for him to marry. You tryna give him one of your nieces? How are you going to pull that off?"

The playful expression that remained on his face from his laughter was replaced with one of seriousness.

"I don't want a niece to marry Carlos; I want you to marry his sister."

The hearty laughter I released brought tears to my eyes. There was no way he was serious about this shit. I had no desire to get married, and I for damn sure wasn't going to get married to someone I didn't even know.

"You're joking, right?" I asked as the last of my laughter died down.

"No, son. I'm serious."

Our eyes remained locked for a while before I damn near yelled, "*Hell* nah!"

"Bay..."

"Nah, Pops. Now, it's a lot I'll do for you and the business, but this ain't it."

He chuckled and shook his head as his tongue rolled over his cheek. "You say that as if you have a choice." I sat back in my seat. "You know family is over everything, and at times, that includes ourselves. You know how much this organization means to me. To us. This is your future. Your legacy. If you do this, it will prove to me that I can trust you to lead my men when I retire. If you don't, I'll make sure what I have *never* touches your hand." Pops stood. "Now I'ma give you twenty-four hours to think on it, though I've already made the decision for you. You're going to marry her, get inside their organization, and learn how it runs. When you're confident you're ready to take over, kill Carlos. I don't care what you do with the girl." He made his way to my side and palmed my shoulder. "Be at my place tomorrow at six for dinner with them, and please, be on your best fucking behavior."

It didn't matter how in control I tried to remain of my emotions. Before I could stop myself, I was standing and knocking everything off the table. All eyes were on me, including Pops'. With a grunt, he shook his head and smiled as he continued out of the restaurant.

Truth was, I knew there was nothing I could do to get out of this. I did want to take over eventually. I also was fully aware that family and this organization meant every-thing. If Pops believed this was the best way to keep Robert's business and please the board, there would be nothing I could do to get out of it. So, as much as I hated the idea of marrying someone I didn't know, I left *At Steak* defeated because that would soon be my future.

Whiskee

I couldn't remember the last time I saw my brother nervous. It made me feel like this was more serious than I'd realized. I felt ill-prepared. His aura was consuming mine like it did when we were kids and he'd done something he didn't want our parents to know about. The weight of that guilt would sit on my heart, and I would do anything I could to protect him and keep his secret, even though he was my big brother. Carlos would always do the same for me.

Convincing myself everything would be okay, I took his hand in mine and gave it a gentle squeeze as he rang the doorbell. Carlos looked down at me and smiled with one side of his mouth.

"I love you, Whis."

"I lo—"

Before I could return the sentiment, the front door was being pulled open. A tall, wide man stared down at me. His frown was replaced with a slow-spreading smile... and it creeped me the hell out.

"Thank you again for setting this up, Tim. I really appreciate it."

Oh, so this is Tim?

His looks in no way hinted at his occupation. The middle-aged man was dressed in a beige suit that perfectly framed his cashew-brown skin. He had a low-cropped curly 'fro that was shiny with a few gray pieces here and there. His eyes were piercing—scary. I wanted to look away, felt like I needed to, but it was like they had me in a trance.

"Your sister is absolutely *beautiful*."

Instead of shaking Carlos's extended hand, Tim outstretched his for mine. I looked over at Carlos, whose bobbing head urged me to shake it. I did, and I had to damn near pry it from his grip. I was already uncomfortable and ready to go home, but I trusted my brother to make sure nothing happened to me.

Tim invited us in, letting us know he'd given his staff the night off, except for the chef and waitress, so we could have some privacy.

Waitress.

The man had a damn waitress at his home.

We made our way through the foyer and down a brightly lit hallway. Carlos and Tim made small talk as I remained quiet, more interested in my surroundings than their conversation. Tim's dining room was large and opulent. In the center of the room was a large dining table that seated twelve people. It was covered with white and cream place settings and candles. Small bouquets of flowers lined the table in between the glasses. A low-sitting chandelier dazzled, and the walls were covered with beautiful art and mirrors.

Once we were settled, the waitress, Ella, came to get our drink orders. They opted for brown liquor and water, and I asked for white wine. She gave me five options and I chose Roscato. It might have been the cheapest one she mentioned, but it was also the sweetest, and that was my preference.

I hadn't been interested in listening to their conversation when Carlos first asked me to come, but after hearing him say Tim said he could be vitriolic, I wanted to be on alert. If at any point I felt like he was disrespecting my brother or my father's memory, I'd shut this dinner down real quick.

About ten minutes passed before heavy steps suggested someone was heading into the room. My head shifted, eyes landing on a fine ass younger version of Tim. He had a tall, more athletic build than his father. They had the same cashew-brown skin. I couldn't see much of his body, but I could tell that his hands, neck, and top of his chest were covered in tattoos because the first couple of buttons on his white and black striped button-down were open.

Tight, golden-brown eyes were just as hypnotic as his father's... but they were less scary.

"You're late," Tim said to the younger version of himself as he stood.

"You want me to handle business, or you want me to be on time?" he asked, shaking Tim's hand.

"I want you to do both," Tim replied with a warm smile —a genuineness I hadn't felt since we'd arrived.

When Carlos stood to shake his hand, I tried to mimic the gesture. Stepping in front of me, he lifted his hand, stopping my movement.

"Stay seated," he commanded in a voice softer than the one he'd used with Tim. With my hand in his, he looked at me with those piercing golden-brown eyes, and with each passing second, I felt more and more under their spell. "Beethoven Smith, but everyone calls me Bay."

"Hi. Whiskee."

"I wish the circumstances were different, but it's nice to meet you, Whiskee."

"You as well," I agreed, releasing his hand.

Seemed he didn't want to be at this dinner either.

Beethoven made his way around the table, and I couldn't stop myself from watching his every step. The black slacks on his legs had to be custom-made based on how well they fit his sculpted frame. Loafers were on his feet, giving him a casual business vibe that was sexier than I wanted to admit.

He took the seat that was directly across from me, and I hated that. It would be hard for me to keep my eyes off his handsome face. That scruffy beard, those skin-colored and heart-shaped lips... that chiseled jaw and those pointed facial features.

God.

This man was too damn fine for his own good.

Clearing my throat, I forced my gaze away and took a sip of my wine.

It didn't help that he was staring at me just as much as I was staring at him.

To make it even more awkward, Tim and Carlos kept finding reasons for Beethoven and me to engage one another. So far, not one word had been spoken about business. Maybe Tim really did want to get a feel for Carlos and me on a personal level. I started to relax more, hoping the evening would be a success.

Just before our entrees were to be delivered, Ella cleared the salad plates. Tim took that opportunity to privately speak with Carlos, leaving me and Beethoven in the dining room alone.

"Now that we're alone," Beethoven started, "How are you feeling about this arrangement? And please, be honest."

I scratched the back of my head, thinking over his question carefully. With me having no idea what arrangement he was referring to, I shrugged.

"I'm not sure. Carlos didn't share much with me about it."

Scoffing, Beethoven sat up further in his seat with a shake of his head. "And you're cool with being left in the dark? You have a say in this too."

"A say?" Chuckling, I cupped my hands on top of the table. "My father never let me in on his business affairs, and I don't expect Carlos to either. The less I know, the better."

Confusion covered his handsome face. His nostrils flared and brows wrinkled as he frowned.

"So let me get this straight. Your brother tells you that he needs you to marry a man you don't even know, and you just... go along with the shit?"

My heart dropped before it began to beat rapidly.

Marry a man I don't even know?

There had to be some kind of mistake.

My mouth opened and closed, but nothing came out. Swallowing hard, I pushed back the emotions that were consuming me as my body swayed in the seat.

"I'm not sure what you're referring to, but I'm not here to discuss marrying *anyone*. Carlos told me he needed to meet with Tim for dinner so he would continue to work with him, that's it."

His body relaxed in his seat. Beethoven released a low hum before chuckling and shaking his head.

"So he didn't tell you?"

"Tell me what? You can't possibly be suggesting the way for Tim to work with my brother is for me to marry someone."

"That's exactly what I'm saying," he spoke through gritted teeth, fisting the table in a way that made me jump. "My father wants us to get married so y'all will be considered family. That's the only way he will work with your brother."

"And Carlos knew about this?"

Beethoven's head shook as he sat back in his seat. "Yeah. I thought you knew too."

Finally... everything started to make sense. Why Carlos gave very little details about this dinner meeting. Why he kept telling me he loved me and wanted me to remember he did everything for me. Why Tim kept shooting conversation topics me and Beethoven's way.

"That fucking *bastard!*" I seethed quietly, hopping up from the seat so quickly it almost fell backward.

If I was to be used and betrayed by anyone, I wouldn't expect it to be my brother... the only person in my family I had left. Especially so soon after we lost our father. All of that was the truth, and now that I was aware of it, Carlos had a hell of a lot of explaining to do.

Beethoven

I felt bad for Whiskee.

I thought she knew about the arrangement; otherwise, I would have kept my mouth shut so her brother could tell her. She needed to know, though. I was confident Pops and Carlos were somewhere finalizing the details of the agreement.

Whiskee was beautiful, which made this evening harder than I thought it would be. No matter how much I tried to avoid talking to her, Pops kept forcing conversation between us. Whiskee was cool. She had a calm spirit—until now. She was shaking as she stormed out of the dining room and she had every reason to be upset.

It was one thing for my father to ask this of me because I was in the business and dedicated to doing whatever it took to ensure it continued to flourish. From the sound of it, Whiskee didn't have anything to do with the business. It wasn't fair for her to be forced into this life, whether it benefited us all or not. If she wasn't willing to do this on her own, I would not force her to.

I stood and headed in her direction just as she whimpered and covered her face. "I don't even know where to go," she said into her palms.

Lowering her hands, I held the left one. "Follow me."

Each time she sniffled, that shit was like a shot to my heart. I looked down at her just as she quickly wiped away a tear. Jaw clenched, I tightened my grip on her hand. Forcing her into a marriage without her permission was some true bully shit... and I'd *never* liked bullies. I shouldn't have been surprised, though. Pops probably told Carlos not to tell her. He liked to be in control.

I led her to my father's office. Without knocking, I opened the door. Whiskee was like a little tornado as she made her way inside. Carlos stood immediately, tossing a nervous smile her way.

"Hey, sis, I..."

She slapped the spit out of his mouth.

"*Damn!*" I yelled, covering my mouth and my laugh.

Pops lowered his head, fingers pressing into his desk as his shoulders shuddered from his quiet laughter.

"Are you out of your fucking *mind!*" she roared as Carlos gripped his cheek and stared down at her with a frown. "There's no way in *hell* I'm marrying this man! I don't even know him! How dare you bring me here without telling me the whole truth!" She chuckled, crossing her arms as he took a step back from her. "Oh, I know why. It's because you knew I would say no."

"All right, that's enough," Pops said. "Simmer down so we can talk like adults."

"Now you want to talk like adults instead of making decisions for me like I'm a child?"

"Whoa," Carlos said, gripping her wrists and standing

directly in front of his sister. "Pipe down, sis. That's not the man you want to disrespect."

"Neither of you have respected me in this situation, so I'm not giving my respect. I can't believe you, Los. How could you do this to me? Daddy hasn't been gone for but six months and you're already acting like a person I don't even know!"

"Sit down, Whiskee," Pops ordered with a firm tone.

When she didn't make a move, I walked behind her. If I was the only person on her side with this, maybe I could help keep the peace. With her wrist in my hand, I told her, "Let's sit down so we can keep this from escalating, okay?"

She stared at me for a few seconds before her body softened and she nodded. I led her over to the four leather chairs that were in front of Pops' large wooden desk. Instead of sitting next to her, I stood behind her. Quite frankly, I didn't trust either of them with Whiskee, and if needed, I wanted to be able to get her out of here quickly.

Whiskee looked up at me with watery eyes and gave me a soft smile.

Pops sighed as he took his seat. Carlos sat down as well. He didn't sit in the seat that was next to Whiskee, and that made me smile. So did the red print on his cheek.

"You're upset because you were left out of the conversation," Pops said, cupping his hands on the desk. "I get that. It wasn't our intention to make you upset. We wanted to get the details squared away before we brought you in. Now that we have, your brother can tell you everything freely."

Carlos picked up where Pops left off. "I told you how important it was for us to stay in business with Tim, and I also told you Pops was the only man he did business with that isn't in his family. In order for us to maintain our business relationship, we have to be considered family, Whiskee."

"Then do business with someone else."

"I can't. The strain that Tim produces for us is one of a kind. Our clientele pays what they pay because of it. If I switch the product, I risk them not being satisfied and going elsewhere. On top of that, Tim discounts the product because of how well our sales are. If I go to a different supplier, I'll end up spending three times as much for product that isn't as good or strong. And if I tried to grow it myself, not only would I have to wait for the harvest, but I'd have to spend a hell of a lot of money that we don't have to spare for production. That was never Pops' desire. We don't have a choice, sis, and I need you to understand that."

"Whether you understand or not," Pops said, "This is happening." He slid a folder in her direction. "We just signed the contract. Though... after seeing how beautiful and fiery you are, I wish I would have kept you for myself."

Whiskee snatched the folder up, and I read over the contract as I stood behind her. Sure enough, he and Carlos had outlined their business arrangement based on our impending nuptials. We were required to be married by the end of the year, or sooner depending on the needs of both families, or the agreement would be over. Both signatures tonight meant Carlos would be able to leave here and secure the product that had been sitting for the last six months.

"I advise the two of you to talk and come up with your own set of boundaries, rules, and expectations," Pops continued as he stood. "Carlos and I have more to discuss." When Whiskee remained silent as she continued to read, Pops chuckled and continued. "Bay, take your wife home, and make sure she understands tonight will be the first and last time she *ever* disrespects me."

"Sis," Carlos called, trying to hold her hand but she snatched it away. "I'm sorry, but I'm doing what is best for us."

"I hate you," she muttered through gritted teeth as she stood.

"I'll take you home," I offered, placing my hand on the small of her back to remind her that I was here. That she had someone in this room that was just as fucked up behind this as she was. That she had someone in her corner.

"We can talk when I get home," Carlos said as we left the office.

Her head shook but she remained silent. I was glad I drove instead of using our car service tonight. Once we made it outside, I opened the door for her, and she slipped into my silver Porsche 911 effortlessly.

"I don't want to go home," Whiskee said as soon as I got inside.

"Okay. Where can I take you?"

She rattled off an address that was close to forty-five minutes away, then we headed that way in silence. Well, aside from the music that played in the background. Her perfume enveloped me. The vanilla scent was sweet and spicy at the same time. I kept taking deep pulls, somehow soothed by the sensual embrace. When we pulled up to the complex, I walked her to the front door of apartment 1120.

"Whose house is this?" I asked as she stepped closer to the door. "Are you safe here?"

Whiskee nodded, avoiding my eyes. "Yes. This is my best friend's home. I'll be good. Physically at least."

"Take my number. I'm on your side, Whiskee."

Whiskee considered my words for a while before handing me her phone. After I gave it back, she surprised me by giving me a hug. I couldn't imagine how hard this was for her. I was angry when Pops first came to me about it, but Whiskee was angry and hurt. She had every right to feel all that she felt, but I would have to make sure she understood how dangerous it was to disrespect my father. He took that from no one and would kill her in the blink of an eye if she did it again. And for some reason, the thought of that angered me and made me want to protect her more.

Beethoven

I didn't express how I felt to Omari. He was my cousin, my right hand, but his devotion to the business kept me from being vulnerable with him. Regardless of how I felt about it, Omari would agree this was for the best. Tonight, I didn't need someone to tell me my father was right. I needed someone to tell me that regardless, I had the right to feel just as fucked up as I felt.

All it took was one text in our group chat, and they all pulled up. We met at Bully's home because his fiancée, Innvy, was out with Merc's fiancée, Neo, for girls' night.

"So you telling me you actually agreed to this shit," Asylum said. I wasn't surprised he was against it. He'd been married to a woman he didn't love for twelve years and was now with his true love—Dauterive. After spending all of that time apart, Asylum didn't believe in wasting time being with someone you didn't really love or care about and see a future with.

"From the sound of it, he really didn't have a fuckin' choice," Merc replied.

"Everyone has a choice," Bully said, rolling up a blunt. "He made a choice, and that choice was the business and his father's approval. The consequence is a marriage to a woman he doesn't know."

"That's true," I unfortunately agreed. "I can be okay with this eventually. What's fuckin' with me is the fact that Whiskee genuinely had no idea what was going on. They signed the contract and told her afterward. That broke something inside of me. She could give me hell throughout this whole thing simply because of how she was forced into it, and I couldn't even blame her. They really took away her choice in the matter, and y'all know how I feel about that bully shit."

"Damn," Merc muttered. "Hopefully, y'all can talk and become partners in this. I'm sure it really hurt her for them to handle her that way. She's going to need you, Toe. Don't let her push you away."

"Where she at now?" Asylum asked.

"With her best friend. I didn't want to let her go, but I know she needs space to process this."

"You like her, Toe," Bully announced more than asked.

That was his thing. He swore he was a love whisperer or some shit. Even when we denied or couldn't accept how we felt about someone, Bully did. Merc was the one to be supportive no matter what, even if you were going against what you truly wanted. Asylum would keep it real about what you truly needed. I had a solid circle of brothers that I was grateful to God for. I may have been the only one still in the streets, but my crew was very much about that life. It was nothing for us to pull up for each other.

My head shook, but I couldn't open my mouth to deny the claim. She was beautiful, that could never be denied. Her skin was the same shade as whisky, and the yellow dress she had on tonight looked so damn beautiful against her smooth brown skin. Whiskee was short and curvy. I loved that shit. Regardless of how much I tried not to look, my eyes kept lowering to her ass. She had big, doll-like eyes that were so dark they almost looked black. Round lips were covered in red lipstick that matched her nails. As far as arranged marriages went, it could have been a hell of a lot worse.

"Nah," was what I said, but I felt my lips lifting into a smile. "I mean... I like the way she looks... yeah. She's beautiful. Very beautiful. And I feel drawn to protect her, but that's about it." They all looked at each other before laughing, causing me to say, "Mane, fuck y'all," which only made them laugh harder. As much as I didn't want to, I joined in, grateful for the release. It was exactly what I needed tonight.

My phone vibrated in my pocket. When I pulled it out and saw it was a text from an unknown number, I knew it was Whiskee. She was the only person who could be texting my personal line.

> 901-550-9881: Thanks for tonight. I never asked how you felt about everything. This affects you too. – Whiskee

> I don't like it or want to do it, but I'm dedicated to this life and business so I'm down for whatever.

I thought about it for a while and double texted, which was something I never did.

> Having a temporary wife that's as sweet and fiery yet beautiful as you helps.

41

> **Whiskee:** 🙂 You're sweet. Thank you for being so kind. If you weren't there, I probably would have lost it.

> I meant it when I said I got you. Get some rest. We'll talk tomorrow.

> **Whiskee:** . . .

Instead of replying, she hearted the message and left me on read, which was cool. I didn't really want to get close to her. I didn't know how long this would last. Pops said he'd have our attorney email me a finalized copy of the contract in the morning, and I'd look everything over then. For tonight, I needed to sit with my thoughts and feelings so they wouldn't consume me. At the end of the day, this was a business arrangement, and I would have to treat it as such.

Whiskee

I 'd just finished telling Mahogany everything and her response was, "You're joking, right?"

All I could do was shake my head. We were in her bed, and I just wanted to crawl under it and never come out. I couldn't believe the drastic change my life had taken in such a short amount of time.

"I wish."

"You can get out of that contract. It was drafted and signed without your consent. There's no way they can uphold that."

"I was thinking about that, but I don't know, Mahogany. As much as I hate what Carlos has done, I'm not sure fighting it is wise. If this is the only way Tim will work with him, I might just have to suck it up and do it. I'm used to this lifestyle and don't want to be the reason he and I can no longer enjoy it. Now I hate never working or taking care of myself. I feel stuck and don't know what to do."

"That's not an excuse to go through with this, sis. That's

43

not a reason for you to be used and taken advantage of. If you don't want to do this, don't do it. But if you do it... I'll support you."

"Thanks, sis. I'll get through it. Thankfully, Beethoven is cool. Right now at least. I got a lot of guards up with him, and I don't see that changing, but he had my back tonight which I appreciated."

"Is he cute?"

Her syrupy smile led to her biting down on her lip, making me laugh. Mahogany was such a horn dog. I loved how sexually free she was, though.

"He's cute. He's fine as hell, actually."

"Well, there is a bright side to this." I chuckled though she was serious. "And he was nice to you, so that's a plus."

"Yeah, I've been texting him, but I stopped. I don't want to get attached to him and feel closer to him than I should because of the situation. At the end of the day, this is business. And as much as I hate it, maybe it's time for me to step up." Sighing, I looked out of her darkened window. "I've been taken care of my entire life. If this is what I have to do to honor my father's memory and help my brother, I will. I just hate that they took away my choice."

"I can't imagine. I'm sure it would have been different if they would have talked to you about it and asked you first."

"Right! The decision being made for me is what hurt the most. Daddy *never* would've done that."

"Well, he's gone, Whiskee. This is Carlos now, and that man is going to do whatever he wants to do, regardless of how you feel."

"That's what scares me. If this is what he's doing now, I don't want to see how things progress the longer he stays in control."

"Uh oh. What does that mean?"

I didn't answer her right away. Up until now, I was content with staying with my brother forever... or... at least until I was married. Now, I needed to get away. After watching my mother be murdered, I never wanted to be alone. I didn't feel safe in my own home. There were some images you couldn't get out of your head—and seeing a gun aimed at your mother's head while you both were hog-tied was one of them.

But now, Carlos had tainted my trust in him and broken our bond. I didn't want to be around him, and I certainly didn't want to live with him. Maybe that would change in the future, but for right now, I had to start figuring out how to do life on my own. Even if I had to do it in fear.

"It means I need to move out and take care of myself."

"You sure you're ready for that, Whis? If not, you know you can always stay here with me. I know how what happened to Mama Renee has affected you. If you don't want to be alone, you're more than welcome to stay here."

I appreciated her offering that without me even having to mention it. That was why Mahogany was my soulmate. My *sole* mate. The person God designated for me to walk through life with.

"That would be really, really great," I said as my eyes watered. "And I won't be here forever. Just... long enough to get on my feet and get used to the idea of living alone."

"Oh stop. Stay here for as long as you need to. We're a package deal. My future husband will have to get used to us always being together anyway."

Lord knows I needed the light turn our conversation had taken as she hugged me. I wasn't sure how this arranged marriage would work, and honestly, I didn't want to try and figure it out tonight. Tonight, I only had enough energy to wrap my mind around what was actually happening.

"Speaking of future husbands, I guess I'll text Beethoven back. The last thing I want is for him to think I'm rude or angry with him. We need to be allies. If I can't trust anyone else, I need to be able to trust him."

As I started to text out a message, he called me. I was frozen as I watched the call come through. At the sound of my gasp, Mahogany looked down at my phone.

"That's him?" she confirmed.

I nodded, blinking slowly.

She accepted the call and lifted the phone to my ear. Clearing my throat, I ran my hand down it and tried to force something to come out.

"H-hello?"

"It seems like you struggling over there with what you want to say to me. You good?"

As much as I didn't want to, I smiled. "Yeah, I'm good. And you're right, I didn't know what to say. I just... felt the need to say something."

"You don't have to say anything, Whiskee."

The sound of him saying my name made my heart skip a beat as my eyes closed. Pulling in a deep breath, I tugged my bottom lip between my teeth.

"I do. I um... I think we should maybe figure out how we can be allies. You were upset about this too, maybe not as much as me, but still. I don't see myself talking to my brother or your father about this any time soon."

"I agree. How about I scoop you for breakfast in the morning and we can go over a few things?"

"That'll work. What time?"

"Will you need to go home and change first?"

"Nah. I have clothes here."

"Cool, then eight. Does that work?"

That was a little early for me. Since I didn't work, I

usually didn't get up until after ten. I was sure he had tons of things to do, so I agreed. After disconnecting the call, I put my phone on the charger with a smile on my face. For some reason, the thought of seeing Beethoven in the morning made me happy.

 Whiskee

My energy shifted. Sleeping on everything didn't make me feel better; it made me feel worse. I woke up angry. Angry at Carlos and Tim. Angry at this situation. Angry at the fact that my first marriage was a damn business arrangement.

Mahogany was on her way to her office, where she filmed a lot of her brand videos, when she stopped in the guest bathroom and asked, "You need me to bring you anything back?"

Shaking my head, I pulled my hair up into a loose ponytail. "I'm good, sis. Thanks."

"All right. Call me when you get back from breakfast and let me know how it goes. I can't wait until I get back home to hear about it."

Chuckling, I nodded my agreement, and she left me alone. It was cooler today than it was yesterday, so I dressed in a white sweatsuit and a pair of red heels that matched my nails and Birkin bag. The excitement I had about seeing Beethoven had turned into dread. Were we really about to discuss a marriage of convenience like our lives were the topic of a damn romance book? My head shook as I applied my lipstick. All I could do was laugh in disbelief.

As I layered my two perfumes for the day, the doorbell rang. My heart dropped instantly as I clutched the edge of the sink.

He was here.

Pulling in a deep breath, I looked myself over once more before cutting the light off and heading out of the bathroom. The steps became harder and harder to take as I neared the living room. No matter how much I kept telling myself Beethoven was in the same position as me when it came to this, I couldn't deny the fact that he was more willing to go along with this charade. I wanted to be upset that he could have agreed to the marriage, but I was grateful he did. Otherwise, the tension between us would have been horrible.

When I opened the door and saw him behind it, I smiled. Genuinely. All the ill feelings that flooded me seemed to go away with each second that passed of me being in his presence.

Beethoven was dressed down today in jeans and a black sweater. He looked just as good, though.

"Hey, you ready?"

"Yeah."

With one bob of his head, he took a step back so I could step out. After locking up, I followed him to a black town car. Didn't surprise me that he wasn't driving today. Robert Carter never drove himself when he was handling business.

Beethoven waited until we were in the back seat of the car to ask, "Were you able to get some sleep?"

With a shrug, I looked out of the window. "For the most part. You?"

"Yeah."

"Do you have a particular taste for anything?"

"I'm not usually up this early, so I don't really eat breakfast."

On an average day, I would have gotten up and did a little reading then worked out and had a protein smoothie that would hold me over until lunch time.

"Why you ain't say that?"

Chuckling, I finally looked over at him. He looked genuinely upset. "I figured you had a lot to do today, so I didn't want to be difficult."

"I do, but we could have pushed it back and did lunch or dinner."

"Do you actually eat when you're handling business, Beethoven?"

Him not replying right away was all the answer I needed. "That's not the point."

I chuckled, and he smiled.

"Waffle House is fine. I can at least eat some hashbrowns."

"You sure?"

"I'm positive."

"Aight, cool." He told the driver to take us to the nearest Waffle House, which I appreciated.

Silence found us, which was fine with me.

When we arrived, it was Beethoven who opened the door for me. He did the same when we walked inside the restaurant. Instinctively, he put me on the right side of him as we passed a group of men, keeping me away from them. Little things like that made me feel more comfortable around him.

A waitress walked over to our table almost immediately. I didn't mind her smile and googly eyes as she stared at

Beethoven. He was a very handsome man. And he smelled good too. I loved the fresh scent of laundry. Nothing was better to me than cuddling up with a blanket fresh out of the dryer and inhaling that clean scent. That was what Beethoven smelled like, and I think the fresh and clean scent of his cologne was what made me hug him last night.

She took our drink order for coffee and orange juice. Beethoven knew what he wanted shortly after, and since I was only going to get hashbrowns and a side of sausage, I was ready when she came back. Less than fifteen minutes later, our food was coming out. Beethoven went ahead and paid her so we could have some privacy for our conversation.

But we didn't need the privacy.

He got a phone call from his father that demanded his attention.

Three minutes later, a Sprinter was pulling up and parking next to the town car.

"I apologize but I have to go take care of some shit," Beethoven said. "Stay and eat. Reggie will take you back to the apartment."

"Oh, o-okay."

With haste, Beethoven made his way out of the booth. He placed a quick kiss to my temple before jogging out of the restaurant and hopping into the Sprinter. Before the door closed, I saw glimpses of men in all black and masks.

The sight made me shiver.

For a while, I forgot who these men were. Regardless of how nice Beethoven was, he was the heir to a drug organization. I didn't know of his reputation, but he was probably just as dangerous as his father was. That truth didn't make me feel as if I was in danger with Beethoven. If anything, it made me feel safer.

Beethoven

T hree Days Later

THIS WAS THE FIRST EVENING IN SEVENTY-TWO HOURS that I wasn't working. Being a stand-in for my father didn't mean I did nothing. In fact, I did almost as much as he did. His right hand was aware of his role and responsibilities. There was a difference between his advisor and right hand or second-in-command. On the off chance something happened to my father, they wouldn't take his place—I would. So I didn't have to just be with him, I had to learn him and how he operated.

I also was the point of contact for our lieutenants, so whatever issues were going on with production, our workers, money, or customers, the issue came to me first to be screened. If it wasn't serious enough for Pops to handle personally, I took care of it with Omari, and we both were in need of a night out after the bullshit we'd been called in to take care of.

Since I shared with Omari the decision that had been made, we hadn't really had time to talk about it... until tonight. I could tell he was hesitant to ask me about it by how he pushed his glass from one side of the table to the other as he asked, "We just not gon' talk about this?"

"About what?" I asked, though I knew exactly what he was referring to. I just wanted to hear him say it. To admit that this was real.

"You actually going through with the marriage?"

"I don't have a choice. If I don't, he has to get rid of Carlos, which means we lose millions in profit."

With a sigh, Omari squeezed the back of his head. He didn't seem to be for this, which was a surprise to me.

"I'on know, man. Is it really worth all that?"

"It's not just about the money. This will solidify me as my father's replacement. The other two stand-ins won't matter. Automatically, all of this will belong to me." I paused before admitting, "But being honest, this makes me want to do my own thing. I respect Pops doing whatever it takes to keep the board on one accord, but you know I've never been a fan of that shit."

"I agree. The advisor I can rock with, but having an advisory board for his organization has never really made sense to me. If he's the boss of all bosses, no man should be able to usurp him or undermine his decisions."

"Now that I one hundred percent agree with. That's why even if I do this, it won't be for long. I'll give it a year and take this shit from Carlos, but it'll be a parting gift for Pops so I can do my own thing."

"Damn." Omari's head jerked as if my words struck him physically. "Well, you know I'm down for whatever. If you leave, I ain't stayin' in this shit without you."

I figured that would be the case, but it put me at peace

to hear him say it. Regardless of how I felt about my father's business moves, I didn't think I'd ever want to leave him and do my own thing. Now, I was starting to feel like I had no choice. Between me taking care of mostly everything these days and being the face of the business, I didn't like having to answer to the board. What he'd done to Whiskee with Carlos was like the final straw. Some shit I didn't respect regardless of who was doing it, and taking away a woman's freedom in this manner was making me look at him a little differently. I always knew Pops would do anything for his organization and make anyone dispensable, but this was the first time that it ever directly affected me.

The Next Morning

MY TEXT MESSAGES TO WHISKEE WERE GREEN. I DIDN'T think she would block me, but that was how I felt when I called and got an automated message. That didn't make sense. Before going into my mother's home, I decided to call Pops and see if he'd heard from Carlos that he and Whiskee decided to renege on the contract.

"Hello?" Pops answered.

"Did Carlos and Whiskee change their minds?"

"No, why do you ask?"

Deciding not to give him any ammunition, I decided on, "I was just making sure we were still good to go."

"Yeah, we are. He has the product now, so ain't no turning back."

"Aight, Pops. I'll see you later."

After disconnecting the call, I grabbed the doughnuts and coffee and headed to Mama's front door. I had a key, but since she had a lil boyfriend I never used it unless it was an emergency. It didn't take her long to answer, and at the sight of me and what I had, she gave me a wide smile.

"Hey, baby. It's so good to see you."

"It's good to see you too."

She waited until I'd put everything on the kitchen island to pull me in for a much-needed embrace. No matter how old I got or how gangster I was, nothing would ever make me turn away from my mother's hugs and love.

"Is everything okay?" she asked, opening the box of doughnuts. "I haven't heard from you in a while."

It wasn't just work that kept me away. I was struggling with how I would tell her about me and Whiskee. Mama and I naturally had a deeper emotional bond than me and Pops. When I was younger, I resented the way she tried to keep me away from Pops and the business. She tried to shield me from what I felt was inevitable. As an adult, I understood why.

Even if she accepted who my father was and what he was about, she wanted better... something safer... for her child.

I sat down at the island as she placed a doughnut on a plate for each of us. I would've been cool with a paper towel, but Mama was extra like that.

"I'm getting married," I blurted.

Her body wobbled slightly, causing her to grip the island. If this wasn't a serious situation, I would have laughed. No matter how old I got and how much I matured, I was goofy as hell... the one you couldn't sit next to at a funeral.

"Mama."

"You're what? To who? Why is this the first time I'm hearing about this? Is she pregnant?"

"Sit down, and I'll tell you everything."

She did, and I did. The more I talked, the harder her expression became. Even without her saying a word, Mama didn't like what I'd agreed to. When I made the decision, I didn't take into consideration how she'd feel about it. I didn't want her to be upset with me, but it really didn't matter. I had to do what I had to do to help Pops and keep the board from going against us. We needed this money to continue to flow. How we were advancing, my great-great grandkids would be set if I could operate without any distractions for a good three years. Then, I'd retire and never look back.

Sadness covered her face as she pushed the plate in front of her deeper into the island. "Your father has always been a selfish man, but this is just..." Her head shook as she struggled to find the words. "How could you agree to this, baby?"

"It's not just him I have to do this for. The entire board and organization will be affected by the loss too. Plus, marrying her guarantees my position as boss of all bosses."

"And that's what you really want?" Her eyes squinted, and damn looking at me, she peered through me.

With a shrug, I lowered my head briefly. No man could make me fold, but I could never lie or fake the funk with my mama.

"Yeah, it is. It's been my goal."

Her hand covered mine, forcing me to look into her eyes again. "Tell me the truth, Bay. You're holding back from Mama." I didn't respond right away, so she continued. "Your father is greedy. All he cares about is money and power. He says what he does is for the business, but it's for himself. Whatever benefits Tim best, that's what he does. Divorcing him was the best decision I ever made. I wanted you to come with me so badly, but I knew I wouldn't win a fight against your father." She chuckled as her eyes watered. "The day I left, he told me if I tried to take you, he'd kill me."

"*What?*" I almost roared, pulling my hand from under hers. "He threatened you?"

"There's no point in you getting upset about it now. It's done. But if you ever wondered why I didn't fight for you to come with me, that's why. He'd already taken my money and security; I didn't want him destroying our relationship or trying to kill me too. I knew that if I agreed to you staying with him that we would still be able to talk to each other. But even if he let me live, I didn't want him poisoning your head against me or trying to keep you from me."

That shit hurt my heart to hear, and I hated that she'd waited so long to mention it.

"Our marriage was arranged," she continued, "And I need you to promise me that you'll treat this young lady right. Treat her with respect, even if you never love her. She didn't ask for this. Don't make her suffer because of it."

"Hol' up." My hands lifted as I released a low chuckle. "Your marriage was arranged? By who? Grandpa?"

With a nod, Mama released a hard breath. "Yeah. Back in that day, Tim was selling less drugs. The bulk of his money was coming from him being a loan shark and gambling. Dad owed him a significant amount of money." Her shoulders sagged as she released a quick bark of laughter. "He couldn't read, so he didn't see there was a fifty-percent interest clause on the contract. Of course he couldn't pay that, so Tim demanded me instead. It was supposed to be a five-year marriage, but I got pregnant with you, and I couldn't leave you there with him."

"That's why you waited until I turned eighteen to file for divorce?"

Her head nodded and eyes blinked rapidly as she fought her tears. "Yes, it is," she almost whispered.

"Maaa," I stretched, standing. "Why didn't you tell me any of this before now? Ain't no way I would've let you stay in that marriage just because of me."

"And that's why I never told you," she said, using my hand to sit me back down. "I'd do it a million times over if it meant having you and keeping you safe. There's nothing I would change about you, even your father. It's his half of you mixed with mine that has made you who you are, and because of that, I will forever be grateful. I stayed because I wanted to nurture you and give you as much of a shield against your father as I could. I knew you'd have some ways like him but your heart..." She placed her hand on my chest. "Your character, it's different. I'm grateful to God for that."

Now that I was aware of their marriage being arranged, it made a lot more sense. I never felt the love between them, and that was why. Though I hated she stayed for as long as she did for me, I was grateful for it. If she hadn't, ain't no doubt in my mind that I'd be a bad mothafucka if only my father had raised me. Pops taught me the business and how to be a man; Mama taught me compassion, consideration, empathy... how to treat a woman and be a gentleman.

"Thank you for the sacrifice, and for sharing your truth with me."

"If you want to thank me, promise that you're going to treat that young lady like the prize she is. Remember, she's the reason you all are able to do what needs to be done for business. If you never love her, always treat her with respect. And when you exchange vows, don't live in a way that will embarrass her."

Even though I agreed, the thought of Whiskee having a life, a marriage, like my mother's didn't sit well with me. If I couldn't love her, I didn't want her—not for life. We'd have to get Pops to agree to this marriage lasting for just a few months, no more than a year. I wouldn't hold her hostage and keep her from being found by a man who could give her the love she truly deserved.

True enough, I could provide her with a damn good life materialistically and financially, but Mama was proof that shit didn't fill your heart or keep you warm at night. Whiskee deserved better, and I wouldn't be the man that stood in the way of her having that.

Beethoven

I couldn't resist pulling up on Whiskee after I left Mama's home. It wasn't sitting well with me that my texts and calls weren't going through. As I knocked on the door, I hoped she was there, or at least her best friend. Even if she didn't want to talk to me, I needed to make sure she was okay.

It didn't take long before I heard the door unlock. A tall, pretty modelesque woman opened the door. She eyed my frame slowly with a smile, and I couldn't lie, I did the same to her.

"Hi," she greeted, leaning against the doorframe. "How can I help you?"

"I'm Whiskee's husband. Is she here?"

A gasp escaped her as she clutched her chest, and the gesture made me chuckle. Her grin was wide as she nodded.

"So *you're* Beethoven?"

"Bay or Toe," I clarified. Crossing my arms over my chest, I asked her, "What has she said about me?"

She laughed. "All good things... all things considered." I

nodded, pleased with that. "Take care of my best friend," she demanded softly, pushing herself off the doorframe. "Regardless of who her father and brother are, Whiskee is not about that life. Please, keep her safe."

"I will. I give you my word."

That seemed to be good enough for her. She gave me a smaller smile before telling me I could come in. As she walked down the hall, she yelled for Whiskee. I took in the difference in their stature and appearance. Ol' girl had a dancer's body—slim, toned, not really shapely at all. Whiskee was short and slim-thick. They both were beautiful, but I loved the delicacy of Whiskee's features. I bet they had niggas damn near breaking their necks trying to get a good look at them when they were out together.

As Whiskee entered the room, I stood. Even dressed simply in a boxer and crop top set, she looked amazing. That small waist and wide hips combo was going to be the death of me. Every time I saw her, it got harder and harder for me to keep my hands to myself.

"Mahogany almost took you," she said with a smile.

"She's beautiful, but no one could take me from you."

We sat down next to each other on the black sectional. "I know what's on the line, so I was just teasing."

I wanted to tell her business wasn't the reason I said that, but I kept that truth to myself.

"What's going on with ya phone?" I asked. "You blocked me?"

"Oh, no. Not at all. I haven't been talking to my brother, and since our phones are on the same plan, he cut it off. He said since I wasn't talking to him, I can't talk to anyone." Her eyes rolled as she sat back in her seat. "I left the phone at the house when I grabbed a few things this morning and forgot to get your number to put it in my new phone."

"That was some bitch ass shit." I didn't care if he was her brother or not. "This how he regulates his emotions on the regular? Like a petty ass child?"

With a sigh, she ran her fingers through her thick, long hair.

"Not all the time. Just when he's really upset and can't get his way. Not everyone can get this kind of reaction out of him. Just those he truly cares about."

I tucked that information in my mind as I nodded and handed her my phone. "Put your number in there. Now that you're going to be attached to me, you need to communicate with me. I need to know you're safe at all times."

I expected her to give me attitude, but she didn't. Whiskee nodded her agreement and gave me her phone so I could put my number inside. After that, I headed out. I needed to check with the money man and make sure we were back on track now that Carlos had his product. If not, this arranged marriage was going to be a waste.

Whiskee

T hree Days Later

> **Mr. Smith:** I apologize for not being present. I know we have a lot to discuss. Business has been crazy right now.

> Thank you for apologizing but you don't have to. I get it.

> **Mr. Smith:** Thank you. Can I pull up tomorrow? We can go over those boundaries and expectations Pops discussed.

> Yeagf

THE SOUND OF BANGING AGAINST THE DOOR CAUSED MY finger to slip. Jumping up in bed, I rushed out of the room to see what the hell was going on. By the time I made it to the living room, Mahogany's door was being kicked in.

At the sight of Carlos and two men I didn't recognize, I

bounced between amusement and anger. The audacity of him to not only disrespect Mahogany's home but walk in so casually.

"It's been a week," he said, checking the time on his phone. "Tim is on my ass about this wedding. He said you and Bay taking y'all precious time with the plans. That changes now."

"I don't know what the hell has gotten into you but..."

"You need to come home, Whiskee. Now."

"No, you need to tell these big ass niggas to put that door back up. You been acting real brand new lately, and I don't like this shit at all."

"It don't matter if you don't like it; you gon' respect it." Scoffing, I crossed my arms over my chest as Mahogany wrapped her arm around my waist. "Now we can do this the easy way and you get your shit and come home willingly. Or we can do it the hard way and have them carry you out."

"I'm not leaving."

With one bob of his head, both men headed in my direction.

"Is he serious right now?" Mahogany yelled, tightening her grip on me.

It didn't matter. While one of them dangled me over his shoulder like I was weightless, the other shoved Mahogany down the hall and demanded she show him where my things were. No matter how much I fought against him and yelled, I was no match for him physically. It took little effort for him to not only carry me out of the apartment but hold me in the back seat while the other goon drove.

"I hate it's come to this," Carlos said, his head buried in his phone. "The sooner you realize this is for the best, the better."

64

"I'm not your property, Los. You can't kidnap me and force me to do as you please. I don't see why you don't understand that."

"I'm not kidnapping you; I'm bringing you back home where you belong."

"I told you I needed some time. It's bad enough you're making me do this."

"It's not that big of a damn deal. We can get this shit worked out to where you don't even have to live with the nigga. It can be a literal contract only. You might have to make a few appearances with him so their family will believe the marriage is legit and try not to challenge it, but that's it. All that hiding out at Mahogany's apartment is done, though. You making me look bad. If y'all ain't married by the time I need my next shipment, Tim is going to cancel the contract. He threw some bullshit in the game talking about he doesn't want to keep supplying me and you decide to back out. So instead of wanting to wait until the end of the year, he wants it to happen ASAP. I can't let you play with my money, sis."

"You're my brother... not my pimp. Did you forget that?"

"If I was your pimp, I'd be keeping the profit you make off this nigga. At least as your brother, the arrangement I'm making benefits us both. Be strong, Whiskee, and get out your feelings. This is business not personal. You're my sister and I will always love you. I need you to prove the same."

Resisting the urge to spit on him, I decided I didn't want to act as disgustingly as my brother. All he had to do was give me space and time to process the bullshit ass plan he'd pulled me into, and he couldn't even do that.

Now, I didn't care that he was my brother. He was my enemy. And I would treat him as such.

"Whiskee," he called. "I need to know you understand, and that we won't have to have this conversation again."

"I see what it is, brother. We won't ever have to have this conversation again."

The rest of the ride was silent. The goon wouldn't even let me answer my phone as it repeatedly vibrated in my pocket. A cocky smile lifted the corners of my mouth. I knew it was Beethoven, and if he couldn't get in touch with me, he was going to make my brother pay.

When we arrived home, it was even colder than usual. Carlos told me the goons would stay at my door and make sure I didn't try to leave. He said I could leave after Tim was satisfied with the progress Beethoven and I had made. As soon as I was alone in my room, I took my phone out of my pocket and went through the missed calls and text messages. Sure enough, they were from Mahogany and Beethoven. The last text he sent said he was worried and if I didn't respond he was going to track my location and pull up.

My smile returned as I plopped down on my bed and stared at the ceiling.

Little did Carlos know... I'd be out of this room soon...

Beethoven

I was in the middle of a meeting when I texted Whiskee. Omari and I were meeting up with a connect that was from Rose Valley Hills, which was about three hours away from Memphis. He was open to the idea of supplying us if I detached myself from my father. No one in Memphis would work with me because it meant going against him. Having a supplier in Rose Valley Hills would allow me to be close enough to still supply the city, but far enough to not have to worry about their fear of him fucking up our business.

The other good thing about Ike was that he had an importing and exporting business. So if I didn't want to sell directly to customers, I could buy from him and operate as a supplier anywhere throughout the United States. The options of working with someone new were seeming to be endless. The only hesitation I had was being from under my father's protection. He had Memphis on lock, and that included law enforcement. We were able to get away with practically anything because of the men on his payroll and other political connections.

If I removed myself from his covering, it would truly be up to me and Omari to make sure what we built on our own would be just as impenetrable.

When Whiskee sent me that last text, I immediately knew something was wrong. I called and texted her and she didn't answer. Since I'd told her that I needed to make sure she was safe at all times, I felt like she wouldn't have randomly stopped texting me. For a while, I considered that she'd maybe fallen asleep. But that text really bothered me.

I called Merc and got him to track her location through her phone. From the looks of it, she was heading to Eads, which was just outside of Memphis. I knew from a past conversation with Pops that that was where Robert lived. That didn't fill me with relief. If she was going home, she could have told me. I felt like something was off with her bitch ass brother, and I wouldn't be able to rest until I laid eyes on my wife.

I was grateful Ike met us in Memphis because that three-hour drive back home from Rose Valley Hills would have drove me crazy. It took me about thirty minutes to get to Whiskee's location. I hopped out of my Mustang with the quickness and made my way to the front door, not even bothering to check my surroundings. My intuition told me there was no threat here. Not to me at least.

After I rang the doorbell, it took a while before someone answered. When they did, it was Carlos. His eyes damn near popped out of their sockets at the sight of me.

"Wassup, B—"

"Take me to Whiskee," I ordered, stepping inside the home.

"Uh, yeah, sure."

We went down a series of halls and up the stairs before getting to the room at the end of the hall that was being guarded by two men. A laugh escaped me as I rubbed my palms together.

"Y'all know who I am?" I checked. They looked at each other then nodded. "Good. Get lost."

They wasted no time heading down the hall as Carlos yelled, "Aye!"

Ignoring his disbelief, I knocked on the door. Whiskee answered, looking from me to her brother with a smile.

"The fuck you got her locked in this room for?"

"She's been gone for a week. Your daddy has been on my ass about y'all not making no progress. I figured if she was at home, she would start to take this a bit more seriously."

"Whiskee is not to be guarded like this anymore. She can have guards while she's out after we are married, but if I *ever* hear about you keeping her trapped somewhere, I'll kill you." I paused to allow my words time to enter his mind. "And I know about that bitch ass shit you did with her phone. I'm the only person she needs to stay in contact with. I don't give a fuck if she goes a week or a year not talking to yo' ass, you come to me with any issues you have with my wife. Not her. Do you fuckin' understand me?"

His jaw clenched and eyes lowered, but he didn't buck. Instead, he nodded his agreement.

Directing my attention to Whiskee, I asked her, "Do you want to stay here?"

"No," she answered quickly, turning slightly away from her brother.

"Then grab your necessities so we can go."

Her head bobbed and she did as I asked. I waited at the door to make sure her brother didn't try no shit. Pops was right about this mane. He wasn't built to be a leader, and he for damn sure wasn't built to be a boss. At first, I hesitated with the order of killing him. Now, I couldn't *wait* to put a bullet in his ass.

Whiskee

"I'll take you back to Mahogany's place, but I don't like your brother knowing where you are. I'd prefer to get you an apartment," Beethoven said.

He'd pulled into the small set of shops just up the street from what no longer felt like my home.

"I um…" Looking out of the window, I rolled my tongue over my teeth. I didn't talk about what happened to Mama to anyone other than my old therapist and Mahogany. "I've never lived alone, Beethoven."

"By choice or by force?"

His question made me smile. "Believe it or not, my family and I used to have very healthy relationships. Even me and Carlos. He was my first best friend." My smile wavered. "By choice. I… have a trauma that I've kind of worked through, but one of the effects of it is a lack of a desire to be alone at night."

Beethoven surprised me by taking my hand into his. "You don't have to talk to me about it, but it might be good

71

for me to know. I never want to do anything to trigger you, Whiskee."

Looking into those golden-brown eyes hypnotized me like every other time. But this time, there was something else inside his eyes. Something that made me want to lower my walls so he could see me too... just a little.

"Seven years ago, while Daddy and Carlos were out handling business, we were robbed. Mama and I were there alone. It happened in the middle of the night while we were asleep, so we had no time to prepare or try to defend ourselves. They grabbed us out of bed and carried us to Daddy's office, where his safe was. It was like they knew it was there and had been sent by someone specifically for what was inside."

Releasing a shaky breath, I looked out of the window. It was easier to detach from the memory that way. "They tied us up by our wrists and ankles and laid us on our bellies. When they were done cleaning out the safe, they took all of our jewelry. Three of them left, but the fourth stayed behind." Blinking back my tears, I stared down at my hands. "He um... put the gun to the back of my mother's head. As she looked into my eyes with tears streaming from hers, she told me she loved me. I begged him not to shoot her, but he did. Right in front of me. At that point, I wanted to die too."

Chuckling, I wiped away a disobedient tear. "I yelled for him to kill me too, but he didn't. He laughed and said watching her die would be punishment enough for me. So after that, it was hard for me to sleep. And when I could sleep, I didn't like to be in the house alone. I would have night terrors and see that night over and over again."

A smile lifted the corners of my mouth at the thought of, "Daddy would sit in a chair in my room while I slept for quite some time. And that's when I realized I needed help. I started therapy, which did help, but I don't think anyone ever gets over losing a parent—especially so violently. I wouldn't say that I can't live alone, it's just that I haven't tried. With everything going on right now, I don't think I'm in a good enough head space for that right now."

Beethoven opened the door and got out of the car. He made his way to the passenger side and opened the door. After unbuckling my seat belt, he pulled me into his arms and held me. I didn't realize just how much I needed to be embraced until I was enveloped by the warmth of his arms. Tears that I thought I was done shedding released. With a gentle rock, Beethoven held me until I was all cried out. His chin rested on the top of my head as he said, "Now that you have me, you'll never have to be alone again."

We had an expiration date. This wouldn't last forever. Still, I held him tighter, appreciating the gesture. When we pulled away, Beethoven wiped my tears and opened the door so I could get back inside.

"Thank you for sharing that with me."

"Thank you for being a safe space for me to do so."

"I'm going to drop you off and handle something real quick, then I'm going to pick you up for dinner. Your brother may have had a fucked-up way of going about it, but he is right. We do need to stop putting this off."

"I agree, and that's fine."

"Aight, it shouldn't take me more than a couple of hours, but I'll call you when I'm on my way to pick you up."

It was crazy how I didn't know too much about this man, but I was already dreading him leaving and looking forward to his presence again.

Beethoven

I didn't want to believe what my gut was telling me, but if I never listened to anything else Mama taught me, it was to follow my gut. Right now, my gut was telling me Pops knew *exactly* who was responsible for the robbery that killed Whiskee's mother and caused her to live with that trauma.

Pops' house was more like a castle. From the front door, it took me several minutes to make it to his man cave on the lower level of the home. He opted for that instead of a basement, along with a panic room. An evening spent with his advisors drinking and talking shit felt like a luxury he didn't deserve if what I felt was true, so I didn't mind barging in and fucking up their vibe.

His laughter turned into a comfortable smile as he watched my every move toward the card table they were seated around.

"Y'all excuse my son. It seems Bay has temporarily forgotten his manners."

"I need to talk to you. Right now, Pops."

Releasing an irritated sigh, he puffed his cigar twice and

took a sip of his cognac before he stood and followed me over to the pool table.

"What's this about, son?"

"You remember that robbery from years ago that ended with the victims being tied like pigs?" He confirmed with a nod. "The woman died. You said the robbery was done by someone in our organization. Why?"

As if he knew where I was going with this, he rolled his tongue over his cheek and squeezed the back of his neck. Pops stood on what he did and what he allowed, but there was only one thing he cowered when admitting to, and that was the harming of women or children intentionally with no cause. That was the biggest thing I hated about his style, but it showed no one was off limits and made men fear him more. If they believed no one in their life was safe and that he'd use their wives or girlfriends to make them suffer, they were more likely to do as they were told.

"It was jealousy. They wanted to sit someone down. But shit went left. He wasn't there. His wife and daughter was, though. So they did the robbery anyway."

"And they killed his wife?" I asked, even though I had the answer already. "It was Robert, wasn't it?" Pops nodded. "Who did it?"

His eyes tightened as he glared at me. "Why?"

"Because that shit traumatized Whiskee, and I need to know that the people responsible were handled."

Pops' head shook. "They weren't. They wanted to sit Robert down for a while, and technically, they did. He slowed down to grieve and focus on his kids. Now I don't agree with what they did, but I respect the hustle. By getting him out of the way, they were able to sweep in on his product and clientele. It didn't matter because Robert came back stronger than ever, but still."

Closing the space between us, I gritted my teeth to keep my face neutral. "Who was it, Pops?"

"Your uncle Mario gave the order. Your cousin Malik and some of his old crew executed it." When I tried to walk away, he stopped me. "But listen, I didn't approve of them killing the wife. She nor Whiskee were supposed to be harmed."

"I'm tryna figure out why you approved the shit anyway. If he was your top seller, why would you want to sit him down?"

Pops sighed. "Family is over everything, Bay. Family wanted a chance to step up, and I gave it."

For a while, I could only stare at him. I understood his allegiance to family, but in some instances, that loyalty had to be placed elsewhere. No way in hell would I risk losing my highest earner just because a family member couldn't get their weight up. If that was what it meant to be the boss of his organization, that was another reason for me to stand down.

"Family means nothing if you don't move with honor and integrity. That was wrong, Pops, and since you didn't care enough to handle it... I will."

"Bay..." he called as I walked away, but I ignored him. "Let 'em live!"

Out of respect for him, I'd let my cousin keep his life. But tonight, he was going to learn a lesson that would keep him from *ever* hurting a woman again.

A Few Hours Later

STEPPING OVER MALIK'S COMATOSE BODY, I CHECKED the time on my phone. I told Whiskee I'd take her to dinner, but it was later than I expected. It was more important to me that I handle this, but she probably wasn't going to feel the same way—especially since I didn't plan on telling her what I was doing to be late. Would it give her peace knowing the people responsible for her mother's death were knocking on death's door? I was sure it would. But nothing would bring her mom back.

If she ever expressed interest in vengeance, I'd tell her what I'd done. And if she wanted them dead, family or not, I'd make that happen too.

"You going to your girl looking like this, Toe?" Merc asked as we walked outside.

I looked down at myself, cursing under my breath at the sight of blood splattered over my shirt.

"If I go change, I'ma be even later."

"Come to the crib since it's closer," Bully offered. "We about the same size."

With a nod, I shook his hand. Typically, this was something I'd handle alone, but as soon as I linked up with them and told them about what happened, they wanted to come too. I needed to calm down before going to see Mario and Malik, otherwise, I wouldn't have been able to spare their lives like Pops wanted me to. They didn't spare an innocent woman's life. What made them better than her? Being of the same bloodline as me? That was fucking bullshit.

I didn't want to continue to think about it, or I'd go back and put a bullet between Malik's eyes. He was a bully who felt like he could do whatever in the name of my father and get away with that shit.

"I'on like that look in ya eyes," Asylum said. "That hate still in you."

77

"If you would've saw the way she looked telling me about that night, it would still be in you too," I countered. "Whiskee hasn't been alone at night since. The fuck am I supposed to do with that? I can't protect her from her own thoughts. This shit gon' eat at me."

"You don't have to protect her from her thoughts," Karrington said. "You just have to make sure she feels safe. Safe with you and safe with herself. So safe that no matter the time or who is around her, she will know she will be good."

That, I could do.

I thanked them again before we got into our cars and went our separate ways.

Though Bully offered some of his clothes I decided to go home so I could have some extra time to release what was in my head and heart. Whiskee was doing something to me —pulling out feelings and actions no other woman had before. If she had me going against family now and we hadn't even signed those papers yet, I didn't want to think about what I'd be doing when she finally became my wife.

Whiskee

Darkness came before Beethoven did. I didn't realize I'd fallen asleep on the couch until the doorbell woke me up. I didn't get up right away, thinking it was in my head. The sound of hushed voices caused me to open my heavy eyes. Beethoven kneeled before me, pushing my hair out of my face.

"I'm sorry."

I wanted to tell him it was okay, but it wasn't. I didn't mind him being late, I just wished he would have communicated that he would be.

"Call or text next time."

The left side of his mouth lifted as he smirked and nodded. "Yes, ma'am."

When his hand lowered from my cheek, I noticed it looked different. Sitting up slightly, I took his hand into mine. "Beethoven..."

"It's fine."

My head shook as I noticed the cuts, redness, and swelling. "This isn't fine. Does it hurt?"

"It's nothing I'm not used to, Whiskee."

"It needs to be wrapped so it won't get infected."

I didn't care about his impatient sigh as I stood and used his shirt to tug him toward the bathroom. I made him lean against the counter as I grabbed the first aid kit from the hall closet. From the looks of both hands, he'd washed them but didn't do much else. I didn't see any dried blood, but I also didn't see any remnants of creams applied.

"This is normal for you?" he asked softly as I began to apply a liquid antibiotic on one hand and then the other. "Bandaging battered hands?"

With a chuckle, I nodded. "Unfortunately. Did you forget who my father and brother are?" We locked eyes briefly. "I wasn't in the streets with them, but after fights or a shooting, I saw the effects."

Beethoven stared at me as I wrapped his hands loosely. "You'll still be able to move them around. I want you to apply this solution for the next three days. Rewrap them for the next four nights. Then, keep the gauze off so they can breathe. If it throbs because of the swelling, ice it. Try not to keep it uncovered for too long. It needs this wrap and moisture to heal. Air will just dry them out."

When he didn't respond, I looked up at him to make sure he was listening. Because of how he'd leaned against the counter, our faces were closer. Our lips were closer. So close they touched. So close we kissed. What started as a slow, careful introduction turned into a deep, nasty exhibition as if we'd done this in another lifetime. I couldn't remember the last time, if ever, that a man had kissed me so passionately. By the time he pulled away, I was too stunned to speak or move.

Beethoven stood upright. His body against mine pushed me back gently. Clearing his throat, he ran his fingers down the corners of his mouth as he looked at me with an intensity that sent my heart straight down to my pussy. It melted for him, resting in the seat of my panties.

"Get dressed so we can go."

I nodded and swallowed hard, afraid that... instead of words coming out... it would be a moan.

———

I HAD NO IDEA WHAT BEETHOVEN HAD PLANNED FOR US. Since it was so late, a lot of places were closed. He ended up taking me to his family's restaurant, where the chef prepared dinner for just the two of us. While we ate, we got to know each other a little better. He told me about his parents and childhood, and I shared a little more about mine.

We went over the basics about each other—our birthdays, favorite things, likes, and dislikes. After that, he surprised me by going back to the apartment and picking up Mahogany. Then, he took us to his gun range. He said he wanted to make sure we'd be able to protect ourselves if anything happened and he wasn't around. I appreciated the gesture. I also appreciated the fact that, when we made it back to the apartment, Asylum was there waiting.

Asylum spent the next hour setting up security cameras, a new door that looked impenetrable, and bars on the windows that would keep any unwelcomed guests out—including my brother. Knives and guns were put in every room, and by the time the men were getting ready to leave, I felt safer than I had in a really long time.

"We still didn't talk about the marriage stuff," I reminded him at the door.

Beethoven gave me a sexy chuckle. "Yeah, we didn't

huh? Fuck it. Let's just do it now and get this shit over with."

"Okay," I said with a light laugh.

It was crazy how that was the reason we were together, but it never came up. I was okay with that, but I also had to remind myself this was business... even if that kiss was really, really good.

I went back into the apartment so he and Asylum could talk before he left. When he came back in, we went to the guest bedroom where I'd been sleeping. As he took off his shoes, Beethoven called Mahogany's name. She came and leaned against the doorframe, wiping sleepy eyes.

"Yes, Bay?"

As sweet as she sounded, I heard the irritation in her voice because she was my girl. Mahogany was ready to go to sleep.

"How much is your rent?"

"Why?"

"If she's going to be staying with you, I'ma pay it."

"Beethoven, you don't have to do that," I told him. "I've already told Mahogany that I'll be going half on the rent for the duration of my stay."

Ignoring me, Beethoven continued to stare at Mahogany until she looked at me then said, "It's um... twenty-eight hundred."

"Aight, cool. You got Venmo or Cash App?"

She nodded. "Venmo."

"I'll get the information from Whiskee and send the money for this month tonight. The next time I come over, I'll have the amount for the rest of the year in cash."

"Just her part," she told him, pushing herself off the doorframe.

"Nah, I'ma take care of it all. Now go and get some rest. You look sleepy as hell."

Her eyes rolled playfully as she thanked him and told us both good night.

"Beethoven, you rea—"

His large hand wrapped around my neck. His fingers stroked my jaw. The action silenced me immediately.

"As long as you're my wife, whether the marriage is arranged or not, I'm going to take care of you."

"Thank you," I replied just above a whisper, lowering my eyes to my thigh as his fingers drew small circles across it. "Speaking of which, how long is this going to last?"

He got a bit more comfortable on the bench in front of the bed and ran his hand over the waves in his head.

"I think three months minimum. Six months to a year max. On the off chance anyone wants to challenge the marriage, we need time to prove it's real. I might have a way to get us out of this though."

That caused me to sit up a little straighter. I'd started to like the idea of being attached to Beethoven.

"What do you mean?"

"I agreed to this because I wanted to help my father and take over when he retired. I'm not fully invested in that anymore. The closer I get to being the boss and the more I learn how he will expect me to run things, the less I want to have anything to do with his organization."

"If we don't do this, what will it mean for my father's organization? Carlos is being insufferable right now, but I still want to make sure we're straight. Not just me and him, but the men that have devoted their lives to my father's business too. I don't want to just... leave them with nothing."

Beethoven gave me a soft smile. "That's... very honorable of you. I expected you to be ready to do whatever to end this before it could begin."

"If we would have had this conversation the night of the dinner or even the day after that would have been the case." I paused. "But... I've been taken care of my whole life. I think it's time I look out for others. Plus, as furious as I am with my brother, I can't leave him to do this alone. He's not handling his new position well. And I know you might not like him but—"

"That's putting it mildly," Beethoven interrupted me to say. "Personally, I don't like the way he mishandles, disrespects, and doesn't consider you. Professionally, he's moving like a bitch. He's trying to gain power and respect that he hasn't taken the time to earn. The only reason he's still alive after that stunt he pulled with you is because I don't want to take another family member away from you."

I couldn't respond right away. Carlos's actions made me want to fight him myself, but it was different hearing someone else express their disdain for my brother. Especially when I knew that person could very well end my brother's life and not think twice about it.

"Carlos needs help. If staying in this arrangement will help him and honor the men who chose to stay after my father died, I'm okay with continuing with the marriage. But I do have a request."

He released a low huff and tilted his head. "I feel like I'm not going to like this request but go ahead."

"Look after my brother." Beethoven's head shook as he looked toward the ceiling. "He's never had this much power and responsibility, Beethoven. He doesn't know what he's doing. Daddy didn't train him to take over like your father has been training you. All Carlos has ever done was oversee dealers and handle enemies. He doesn't know how to lead these men and be the boss. Please... help him. For me."

"I'll do what I can, but you need to know I'm planning to leave soon. Once I get things secure in Rose Valley Hills with this new connect, I'm out."

"What will that mean for me and Carlos?"

"The partnership created will still stand. He'll be straight and so will you. I'll make sure you're more than taken care of before I leave."

"Okay," I agreed softly. "Thank you for giving me a heads up. I don't think I could take another person abruptly leaving my life."

"I wouldn't do that to you. I'll give you more than enough time to prepare. It won't be any time soon. I'm going to make sure y'all are straight with Pops before I make that move."

While I appreciated his words, his future plans still left me a little sad. Beethoven had come into my life, and in just over a week, made me feel levels of safety and comfort no other man had before. I felt seen, heard, and taken care of with him, and I didn't want that to end. Still, I'd play my role and let things play out organically. As long as me and my brother would be straight and my father's men would be taken care of, that was what mattered to me most.

Beethoven

Whiskee was growing on me.

The selfless choice she made to continue with the marriage showed a side of her I didn't think existed. That was a sign of true leadership, unlike what the hell her brother had been doing. Like I promised I would, I pulled up this morning with enough cash to take care of their rent for the rest of the year. I made it clear to Pops that if he wanted things with the wedding and marriage to progress that I'd need some time off to prioritize it. He assured me he'd have all business matters forwarded to the other two stand-ins or to Omari for the next several days, which I appreciated.

Now, Whiskee and I were at the pool in their apartment building drinking and getting to know each other better. Her ass in that damn two-piece swimming suit had my dick hard with no sign of relief in sight. Even though we kissed yesterday, I wasn't sure I'd try to take things further. I would never deny that I was attracted to her, but this marriage wouldn't be permanent, so I didn't want to develop feelings that would be.

"What made your mama name you Beethoven?" she asked before taking a sip of her mimosa.

My drink was mostly champagne, but this was what she wanted to drink, so I obliged her.

"She loves classical music and jazz, so she named me after her favorite composer."

"Do you listen to classical music too?"

"Absolutely. I love it. Jazz too. I listen to other shit but that's what I grew up hearing. What about you?"

"I listen to jazz but not classical music, mostly because I've never known where to begin. I love soul and neo soul. My favorite songs come from the seventies and eighties."

"We can vibe out then." I paused before suggesting, "There's a sunset symphony coming up. Maybe I can take you."

"You mean like a date?" she asked softly with a sweet smile.

"I mean... yeah."

"Would that... is that okay?"

Chuckling, I walked over to her as she sat on the edge of the pool. "Who exactly do we have to answer to, Whiskee?"

As my arms wrapped around her waist, hers wrapped around my neck. "No one but ourselves, but this marriage... it'll be fake."

My head shook. "It ain't fake. It's arranged. What I feel for you is very real... even if I don't want to feel it."

She looked away and licked her lips. There was a ghost of a smile on them when she returned her eyes to mine. "And what do you feel?"

"I feel... like I could really like you and enjoy my time with you. I don't want to ignore that."

"I don't want to ignore it either," she cooed, blushing in a way that made my heart skip a beat. "So what do you suggest? We... enjoy each other while we're bound?"

"That's exactly what I'm suggesting... if that's cool with you."

Her head nodded as she bit down on her bottom lip through her smile. "Yeah, I'd like that."

"Cool."

Our lips were like magnets, drawn to each other without much effort. This kiss was just as good as the first, and like the first, it made me want to kiss every inch of her body as my dick hardened.

To cool things off between us, I pulled her into the pool, which led to a water fight that had her squealing and laughing the whole time. When we were done, we went back up to the apartment to shower and freshen up. I was surprised when she offered to fix lunch, but I agreed.

"Do you have any food allergies I should know of?" she asked, walking around the kitchen island in shorts and a hoodie. Her hair was pulled up into a curly bun. I couldn't keep my eyes or my hands off her. "Beethoven."

"Hmm?"

"I said do you have any food allergies?"

"Nah, bae."

"What's your favorite thing to eat?"

When she bent forward to look in the back of the refrigerator, I groaned. "Pussy."

Standing upright, Whiskee looked over her shoulder at me with a smile. "What's your favorite food to eat, sir?"

"Any kind of soul food. For lunch, it doesn't really matter."

"Hmm..." She turned toward the refrigerator again. "There's some shrimp and chicken in here. I can do pasta or chicken over rice. The Mexican kind or with tzatziki and hot sauce."

"If you can make some white sauce that tastes like what I get from Taziki's, I'll marry you right *now*."

"Say less," she agreed with a wide smile. "If it's one thing I can do, it's cook. I love to create and use my hands."

"What else do you like to create?" I asked, accepting the bottle of water she put in front of me.

"Well, my favorite forms of creativity are hair, makeup, and cooking. I love going to painting or pottery classes too."

"Did you go to school for hair and makeup?"

"Yeah, but I never worked in a salon. I have a small clientele of friends, but that's it."

"Is that how you wanted it?"

With a shrug, she nodded as she sat next to me. "I guess. I never had a reason to work, you know? Daddy always took care of me." Her expression saddened. "I regret that a little now. I feel more dependent than I ever have. A part of me wants to get my cosmetology license renewed and open my own salon so that no matter what happens with Carlos and the business I will always have my own income coming in and can take care of myself."

"I can respect that. I'm kind of in the same boat. Everything I have is attached to my pops. All of my legal businesses. When I leave, there's no doubt in my mind he's going to try and push me out because of spite."

"You really think so?"

"Hell yeah. He's all about family, but he believes family should stay together and do what he says no matter what. I don't think he's going to take me leaving to do my own thing lightly. I got enough money saved to rebuild whatever I lose, though. And because it'll be mine and only mine, it won't be a true loss."

"I'm excited for you. You get to step out on your own and do your own thing. You get to recreate your own life. Not everyone gets that chance."

"Maybe not everyone... but you can. And I wanna help. Once you get your license renewed, I'll help you get a building. I want you to know you can be taken care of, but you can always maintain your independence too."

Leaning forward, she gave me a slow, tender kiss that made me bite back a moan.

"You're dangerous."

I didn't have to ask her what she meant. I already knew. She was dangerous to me too.

Whiskee stood and started to fix lunch. While she did, we continued to talk. We discussed our dreams and goals... motivations... hobbies and interests.

By the time she was done, Mahogany had arrived. She confirmed Whiskee would be able to do her makeup that evening before she went live then left us alone.

"I'm excited for you to try this," Whiskee said, placing a plate full of yellow rice and chicken with tomatoes and cucumbers in front of me. It was drizzled with a white and red sauce that looked damn good.

After saying grace, I took a bite and was impressed. The rice was fluffy and moist—the best rice I'd ever had. The chicken was tender. And the white sauce tasted like something I'd get from a halal cart on a trip to New York.

"This the kind of cooking that will spoil a man," I told her. "What else can you cook?"

With a giggle, Whiskee sat next to me with a plate for herself. "Honestly, probably anything you want. Even if I don't know how to do it now, I'm a fast learner."

"This is amazing, Whiskee. Seriously. I need this on rotation weekly."

The more time we spent together and got to know each other, the more I liked her. I didn't know how easy it would be to walk away from her in a few months, but for now, I was going to take full advantage of the time we had together.

Whiskee

ne Week Later

"GIRL, *PLEASE* SHUT UP!" MAHOGANY SAID, AND I HAD to cover my mouth to keep my laughter from bubbling over.

For whatever reason, these women on TikTok set themselves up for her form of tough self-love every Wednesday when she went live. The woman that joined her live was talking about how hard it was for her to move on from her ex because she didn't understand why he broke up with her. It didn't matter what Mahogany said, ol' girl wasn't listening. Mahogany had finally lost her patience with the conversation, and I wasn't surprised.

"If you at the mall and someone punch you, are you going to stand there and say, 'Oh God. Why did you hit me? I can't believe you hurt me. I would never do that to you.' Nah. You gon' get beat up or beat they ass! It's the same way with this. He punched your heart and hurt you, but it's time to move on. Stop worrying about why he did or

92

the fact that you wouldn't do it to him. Take your L and move on."

All I could do was shake my head and chuckle because, even though her analogy was crazy, what she said was truth. The woman was so concerned with being hurt that she wasn't giving herself the space to heal. She was so focused on the past and the old version of him that she was keeping herself in a state of depression.

I waved at her to let her know I was leaving. Since she had a full day of recording brand videos, I'd come up here to refresh her sew-in and do her makeup. When I made it to my car, I checked my phone to see if Beethoven had texted me back. We were talking about needs, wants, and love languages. I wasn't sure when things started to feel more like a real relationship, but that was where we were at with it now, and I was okay with that.

Before I could read his text, I was getting a call from Carlos. I hadn't heard from him since he had those goons carry me out of Mahogany's apartment. I started to ignore his call, but in case something was wrong, I answered.

"Hello?"

"You answered."

Hearing his voice made my eyes water. I'd never gone this long without seeing or talking to my brother. "Are you okay?"

"I miss you."

A sigh escaped me as I sat back in my seat. "Carlos..."

"I fucked up. I know I did. The power got to me, and I started tripping. Can you come home so I can apologize in person?"

I thought it over for a while before agreeing with, "I'll come so we can talk, but I'm not staying there, Los."

"I'll take that. Can you come tomorrow evening?"

"Yeah, I'll see what I can do."

"Aight, Whis. I love you."

"I love you too."

After disconnecting the call, I checked Beethoven's text, and his reply made me chuckle.

Mr. Smith: I want to talk to you about this face to face. We also need to discuss when you'll be serving me my favorite food.

The chicken over rice?

Mr. Smith: Don't be cute Whiskee. You know what I said my favorite thing to eat is.

You've been very affectionate and open lately. I didn't think there would ever come a day where you'd tell me you wanted me sexually.

Mr. Smith: Should I stop?

No. I like it.

Mr. Smith: You gon like this dick too.

Beethoven!

Mr. Smith: Wait until I'm in that pussy. Then you'll really be saying my name.

Get off my phone Bay.

Mr. Smith: I'on want you calling me what everyone else calls me.

Then what do you want me to call you crazy?

Mr. Smith: Beethoven or Baby. Daddy works too.

😂😂 I will see you later baby. I'm about to head home and get ready for the meeting.

The whole time I drove, a smile stayed on my face. This man was something else, and I was starting to like him more and more.

MEETING WITH A WEDDING PLANNER MADE THINGS even more real. This wasn't just a regular wedding planner; this was a wedding planner that had been used by the Smith family for years. She stayed on trends and had a young team behind her, but the sixty-year-old woman hadn't come to play and knew *exactly* what she was doing.

We basically went over color schemes and menu options so she could put together a schedule for us to try and approve certain things. We also discussed venues. When it was over, Mariam told us that Tim wanted the wedding to happen in three months. With it being late March, the idea of a June wedding wasn't bad. I was just surprised he wanted it to happen so soon. I shouldn't have been. After all, this was a business deal, and Carlos made it clear Tim wanted us married before he gave him the next shipment.

However, Beethoven had gotten his father to change his mind about that, which I appreciated. They may not have trusted my brother's leadership, but they trusted my father's men and his clientele, and the product was moving just as well now as it was when Robert Carter was in control.

"How you feelin'?" Beethoven asked, squeezing my thigh as we cruised down the street. "You still down?"

"Mhm." With a nod, I looked over at him and smiled.

This man was sexy as hell. I still couldn't believe he was my man—whether it was by arrangement or not. After all these years of avoiding men who were in the streets, I'd gotten with one of the heaviest hitters of all. "You?"

"I get to have you as my wife. Of course I'm still down."

Every time he said stuff like that, it made me feel all warm and mushy inside. Forget butterflies—this man gave me fireflies that lit me up and made it hard for me to stay in my darkness.

I wasn't sure of our destination. I was perfectly content being a passenger princess. When we arrived at the new supper club off Main that I'd mentioned wanting to go to, excitement bubbled up within me.

"You listen," I cooed.

"Listening is what makes a great lover. I'll always listen to you."

Light laughter escaped me as I unbuckled my seat belt. "I didn't think a man like you could be a gentleman or intentional lover, and I especially didn't think you'd soften when handling a woman. I'm glad I was wrong."

"Ain't no reason for me to be hard toward you, and I won't allow you to be that way with me. Stay soft and feminine for me. That's what attracted me to you."

Looking out of the window, I released a content sigh. He got out and walked over to my side of the car. When I was out, he pressed me against it as he asked, "Have I told you today that you look absolutely beautiful?"

I'd dressed for him. His favorite color was olive green, so I put on an olive-green dress that accentuated every one of my curves.

"Yes, but I won't stop you if you tell me again."

He gave me one of his signature sexy smiles. "You look so beautiful, bae. I can't keep my eyes off you."

"Damn, Bay. This you?"

At the sound of a man's voice, Beethoven turned. He stayed in front of me, shielding me from whoever it was. Once he saw them, his body relaxed, and he stepped next to me.

"Yeah, she is." He took my hand into his. "Isn't she beautiful?" The man whistled as he looked me over with a nod. "Aight, don't look too fuckin' hard."

The man chuckled as they shook hands. "My fault, cuz. She is beautiful though."

"Thank you," I replied, wrapping my arm around Beethoven's.

They made small talk for a minute or two. I tried to walk away, but he held me close. When they were done, we headed across the parking lot toward the entry. Beethoven had made us a reservation, thankfully, because it was packed. The green, black, and gold décor combined with the dark lighting was beautiful. Jazz music played in the background. We were here just in time to hear the live band that was getting set up on the stage.

The hostess led us to a table that was in the corner by the exit door but still close to the stage. Before our waitress even arrived, two drinks were delivered by the bartender.

"I hope it's cool that I ordered for us when I made the reservation," Beethoven said.

"That depends on how well you ordered."

He gave me a cocky grin. "I think I did pretty well. I got us peach cobbler martinis to start. It has Crown Royal peach in it. Give it a try."

Lifting the pretty drink to my lips, I took a small sip. My eyes closed and I smiled as I savored the sweet and slightly spicy drink. "Mm... you did a really great job, baby. This is good."

Whisky was both our liquor of choice, so it didn't surprise me that he'd gone with a drink that had that as a base, but I was surprised he got something that was this sweet. It did a great job masking the task of alcohol, which meant this was a drink that would need to be sipped and not guzzled.

"Whew." Him wiping his forehead of invisible sweat as he relaxed in his seat made me laugh. "I was confident you'd like it, but I was a little worried too."

"If this is how you're starting out, I think you're going to do just fine."

He'd selected fried green tomatoes for the appetizer along with sauteed shrimp that had the same sauce that was drizzled on the fried green tomatoes on the side. I was just as pleased with those.

While we waited on our entrees, we picked up on our conversation from earlier when Beethoven said, "I know this isn't for forever, but I meant it earlier when I said I wanted to know what you want and need from me. How I can keep you happy and make sure you feel loved."

"May I ask why you care about my happiness? These days, people are not partnership-minded at all. They don't want any responsibility in a romantic relationship, and everyone is out for self. The men I've dated in the past have made it clear my happiness is my responsibility. Why is that different with you?"

"You answered your question yourself. You said people aren't partnership-minded and want no responsibility in their romantic relationship. I want the woman I'm with to be happy, secure, and at peace because if she is, that will affect the way she is with me. With the way my life is set up, I have no room for drama, dis-ease, or a bitter and unhappy woman. I also don't have room for anything unnecessarily hard. That's why I said what I said in the car. I'll put forth effort one hundred percent, but if a woman or a relationship is hard to deal with and maintain, it ain't for me."

He paused and took a sip of his drink. "I don't believe in getting into a relationship and not being prepared to truly love someone, and when you love someone, that means you prioritize their needs and happiness. I don't mind taking care of my woman and keeping her happy because I know she will do the exact same for me. We'll take care of each other, and no one will be taken advantage of or lacking."

I was so impressed with his answer, I couldn't respond right away. When I did respond, I told him what I wanted and needed from a man, and he told me the same. We also discussed what we had to offer.

"My femininity, grace, my mind and heart, but most importantly, my partnership," I told him after he shared with me that he had to offer provision, protection, validation, support, and acceptance.

I loved that we both avoided those cliché things like love and respect. Things that should have come naturally. That did lead to us discussing our love languages. Mine were gifts and physical touch, and his were service and physical touch. That explained why things had progressed between us so quickly physically.

Our entrees arrived, and I had to give Beethoven credit. He selected lamb chops with a Grand Marnier honey glaze sauce that was cooked to perfection. I had not one complaint by the time he asked if I had room for dessert, which I didn't. He asked me to dance, and I happily agreed. Near our table, our hands connected. While my arm wrapped around his neck, his wrapped around my waist. Things between Beethoven and I felt so authentic, I almost forgot our upcoming wedding was a ruse.

"If I'm not careful, I think I'm going to fall in love with you," I confessed.

Beethoven's lips curled upward as he closed the space between us. Lifting my head by my chin, he waited until I was looking into his eyes to say, "You might think that... but I know."

Both of his hands went to my waist as we kissed and continued our slow sway. As the kiss deepened, his hands lowered. When his fingers slipped between my ass cheeks and grazed my pussy I whimpered. The low moan he released as he squeezed my ass and swirled his tongue around mine made my pussy throb. This had been the perfect dinner, and I couldn't wait to see what else Beethoven had up his sleeve.

The kiss left me winded. Avoiding his eyes, I pulled in deep breaths as my nipples pebbled.

"Let me see your pretty face," he demanded, voice just above a whisper as he gently tugged my hair out of the way. Keeping it in a firm grip, he released a moan before tugging his bottom lip between his teeth. "I can't wait to watch you cum."

It took everything inside of me not to tell him that we could leave so he could see it right now. As genuine as our connection felt, things were still so new between us. So instead of replying, I wrapped my hand around his neck and lowered his lips to mine again.

Beethoven

Two Weeks Later
Early April

Her name suited her.

Whiskee.

Skin the same shade as my favorite brown liquor. An aura that had become my addiction. An addiction that warmed me and left me drunk off a woman whose time in my life had an expiration date.

I hadn't seen her for a whole week, and I missed her.

She was on her period, and though I told her I didn't care about that shit, Whiskee decided to stay away. I stopped by to see Mahogany and asked her what kind of things Whiskee liked, then had a care package delivered. Her emotional ass FaceTimed me crying and I laughed, which only made her cry harder. It was then that I realized why she wanted to keep her distance. Whiskee was already a little on the emotional side and her being on her period made it worse.

Whiskee was worth the wait though... even if I did feel some type of way about her spending time with her brother. I felt like that would happen, especially since he called her wanting to apologize. I could respect the gesture of him admitting his wrongdoings, so that was a step in the right direction. But I still didn't trust or respect him as a man or businessman, and I wasn't sure if that would ever change.

"I have two cars, baby. You know you didn't have to come pick me up," she said with that beautiful smile lifting those round lips as she walked outside to meet me.

"I know, but I wanted to see you now, not when you got back to the apartment."

Taking her into my arms, I allowed our lips to connect for a slow, tender kiss that made my dick hard. With a handful of her ass, I kept her in place so she wouldn't pull away before I wanted her to. She started giggling, and that was the only reason I pulled away.

"Did you miss me?" she asked sweetly, looking up at me with those big, doll-like eyes.

"You can't tell?"

"Why don't you show me after our date?" She looked back as the front door opened and her brother stepped out. "Carlos wants to talk to you, so I guess it's a good thing that you came here."

I couldn't stop the irritated breath that released. When I told her I'd pick her up and take her to the apartment so she could get ready for our date tonight, I didn't expect her to want me to talk to her damn brother. As far as I was concerned, we didn't have anything to talk about. The wedding was my professional responsibility in Pops' eyes, so he was not expecting anything else from me at the moment. I was glad about that because I wasn't really fucking with his ass right now anyway.

Between learning my parents' marriage was arranged and that he knew about my cousin killing Whiskee's mom, I was looking at him a little differently. I could understand how, during that time, he didn't give a damn about Whiskee or Renee. The fact that he wanted me to marry her, knowing someone who shared the same blood as us was responsible for her mother's death, wasn't something I could easily get over.

I still hadn't told Whiskee about Malik, and I honestly didn't think I ever would. Last I heard, he was still in the hospital in a coma because of swelling on his brain. A part of me hoped he suffered in that state for a good long while for what he did to Renee.

"For what?"

Her eyes rolled playfully as she smiled. "Go in there and see." When I didn't budge, she groaned and wrapped her arms around me. "I think he wants to make sure y'all are okay." Standing on the tips of her toes, Whiskee pulled me down to her for a quick, closed-mouth kiss. "Please, baby."

There wasn't too much I saw myself denying this woman of, so even though I didn't want to talk to him, I agreed. After getting her settled into the car since I kept it running, I headed toward the front door.

"Wassup?" Carlos greeted, arms crossed over his chest.

"You tell me."

His head tilted as he looked toward my car. "My sister seems to like you... for real."

"Is that what you wanted to talk to me about?"

"Yeah." His arms dropped. "I know she's safe with you physically, but is her heart safe with you too?" It was clear Carlos was serious, but him asking me about his sister's safety with me after he forced her into an arranged marriage without her consent or knowledge amused me. "Look... we all we got. That's my baby sister. I just... wanna know she's safe with you."

I ran my hands down my face and grounded myself so we could have this conversation.

"She's safe with me. I like and care about her too. This shit started out arranged with no feelings, but that's not what it is now. I will never do anything to intentionally hurt my wife."

"Is this relationship going to last forever? You want to marry her for real now?"

"We ain't on that. Not right now at least." I didn't want him to think I was playing around with his sister, but I wouldn't dare tell him I didn't plan to be in Memphis long. Even with the marriage having an expiration date and me and Whiskee having feelings for each other, she understood what I was doing with my father and how important it was for me to break free. "We're dating while we're married, but when it's over, it's over."

"Aight." Carlos's head bobbed. "That's all I needed to hear. Thank you."

We shook hands and I headed to the car. I still didn't like his ass, but asking about the safety of his sister's heart was another point in his favor.

BEING A GOOD LISTENER WAS WORKING IN MY FAVOR. I took Whiskee to a trap pottery class that she enjoyed every second of. It was BYOB, so while we sipped whisky and listened to one hit song after the next, we followed the instructor and created some ugly ass bowls. Whiskee swore they'd look better when we picked them up, but I didn't care. As long as she was happy and had a good time that was all that mattered to me.

"Where are you taking me?" she asked as the town car pulled out of the parking lot.

"To dinner, then to the apartment. Unless you want to stay with your brother tonight."

"What if I want to come home with you?" Her hand slipped up my thigh, settling on my semi-hard dick.

"We can *definitely* make that happen."

My hand wrapped around her neck, tilting her head so I could kiss her. Each soft moan and breathy sigh she released made my dick harder and harder. Even if we didn't have sex tonight, I was glad to finally have the chance to go to sleep with her in my arms.

Whiskee

I was in love with Beethoven's home. It was perfect. The gym, movie theater, and game room were calling my name, but I wanted to be in his bed then his heated pool before the night was over. It didn't surprise me that he had a large home, but it did surprise me to see how well it was decorated. The typical bachelor colors of black, brown, and silver weren't used. Each room had its own vibe and color scheme courtesy of Supreme's wife, Nicole.

The last room he showed me was his master bedroom, which had a bathroom, sitting area, and dressing room closet the size of Mahogany's guest rooms. It was olive green and cream, and the plants, aromatherapy mists, and candles immediately gave me a relaxed vibe.

After cutting on the electric fireplace and starting up a jazz playlist that crooned through the speakers in every corner of the room, Beethoven changed the lighting to a dark red.

A low gasp escaped me when he pulled me into his arms from behind. As his lips lowered to my neck he said,

"Nothing has to happen that you don't want to, but I want you naked in my bed so I can finally taste you."

"I want everything," I confessed, holding the back of his neck as the kisses he placed on mine caused my nipples to harden.

"You sure?" His right hand slid between my thighs. "Because I can wait to give you this dick. But I can't wait to have you on my tongue."

It took me a second to respond. I hadn't had sex since a grief-stricken one-night stand that was rough and fast and climactic but not truly satisfying. Not as satisfying as Beethoven's hands felt all over me. As one set of fingers gripped my neck, the other slowly swirled around my clit through my panties. He tilted my head by my neck, and the increase in pressure made me shiver.

"You like that shit, huh?"

Nibbling my bottom lip, I nodded. "Mhm."

"You like being fucked rough too?" When his grip tightened and he pulled me away before gently smacking me against his frame, I whimpered. "Or do you want me to make love to you?"

My pussy throbbed as he licked and kissed my ear.

"If you keep going, I'm going to cum just like this."

"Then cum. And tell me how you want it."

Beethoven's hand moved from my clit briefly and arched my back, pressing my ass directly against his hard dick. This was one time I loved being a woman who could comfortably strut around in six-inch heels. Without them, I'd be too short for this to feel as good as it was. When he returned his fingers to my clit, he began to circle his hips and press his dick against me.

"I... I want you to do both," I moaned, gripping his hand that was around my neck as my body tingled.

Each time his pelvis pounded against me, I unraveled a little more. Deep breaths as I clawed at his hand didn't keep my eyes from rolling into the back of my head. If this man could turn me on this bad with clothes on, I knew I'd be absolutely out of control when there were no barriers between us.

"Baby," I whimpered, feeling those tingles settle at my core.

"Hmm?"

"It's coming."

"Mm..." Beethoven smacked my ass and squeezed. "Give it to me."

And I did.

He held me up... close... keeping me from falling as my orgasm ripped through me. Before I could compose myself, Beethoven was lifting me and carrying me over to his bed. After placing me in the middle, he took off my heels and dress. Slowly, he removed my panties—showing the wetness he'd just created. When he pulled my panties to his nose and inhaled, my eyes fluttered as I pulled in deep breaths.

"You smell as good and clean as I knew you would." Tossing my panties over his shoulder, he spread my legs and pulled me lower against the bed. "I know you're going to taste as good too."

But he didn't find out immediately.

Beethoven took his time touching and kissing and licking my entire body—to the point my breaths came out choppy as my chest heaved when he finally returned to my pussy.

"Bay," I pleaded.

"Look at this pretty pussy."

His nose slid between my lips, and the groan he

released as he sucked my clit into his mouth was enough on its own to take me to the edge.

I underestimated how sincere he was when he said he loved to eat pussy.

The time he spent eating my pussy had tears streaming down my cheeks by the time I finally pushed him away. Between his licks, sucks, and sweet nibbles, I'd cum three times and had to hold back from squirting. Even with me scooting up the bed, his arm wrapped around my thigh and pulled me back. I put my hand on his forehead, and he chuckled.

"Did I say I was done eating?"

"Baby, please. I'm about to tap out and I haven't felt you yet."

The man pouted and huffed like a child, and it was the cutest shit I'd ever seen. I wasn't sure how I'd gotten so lucky in this unlucky and forced arrangement. Beethoven wasn't just thoughtful and considerate when it came to making choices or date nights, he was selfless and attentive in the bedroom too. He wasn't just mindlessly having his way with me. Beethoven paid attention to what my body, my mind, my mouth reacted to—and he gave that until I crumbled.

"You mine?" My eyes were trained on him as he stood and removed his clothing.

His body was the work of art I knew it would be.

Tattoos covered his cashew-colored chest and abs, arms and hands, and his neck. His athletic build was toned with not a percent of fat in sight. But his dick... his dick was thick and heavy... long and curvy... my mouth watered just in anticipation of gagging on his length.

"Whiskee."

I lifted my eyes to his, and those golden-brown piercing

orbs held me captive like they always did. When he smiled, my heart squeezed. This man was going to fucking *ruin* me.

"Yes?"

"Are you mine?"

The sight of him stroking his dick made my legs open and close as I nodded. "Yes," I almost whispered. "I'm yours."

"Because you want to be?"

"God, yes," I moaned, lowering my fingers to my soaking pussy. As sensitive as my clit was, I wanted him so bad I would suffer.

Finally, Beethoven made his way between my legs again. Our lips connected, but I wasn't able to kiss him back as he stretched my pussy. He didn't seem to care. He placed kisses all over my face and neck until he was all the way inside.

He gave it to me how I wanted it—rough and slow, long strokes that allowed his head to graze my clit before he slid back inside deeply. While one hand dug into his ass and asked for more, the other clawed at the headboard to keep me from sliding up it. Each stroke rocked my body. Even if I wanted to savor it and not cum quickly, that wasn't an option. I didn't just cum; I gushed all over him.

As he released curses and moans of his own, Beethoven wrapped my legs around his waist and softened his strokes. They went just as deep as he picked up a medium pace, but they weren't as hard. His tongue swirled around mine at the same pace of his strokes, being interrupted at times by moans and whimpers or me calling his name.

Somewhere around the third position, our eyes locked as he slowed his pace. Those gentle strokes had my chin and lips trembling as the sound of my wetness covering him filled the room and mixed with the jazz playlist. When I told him I wanted him to make love to me too, I hadn't taken into consideration how that would feel within my heart. How careful he would be. How intentional he would be.

My head shook as I snapped my eyes shut and tried to push him away, but that didn't work.

"Stay with me," he pleaded, lifting my hands over my head with one of his. "I'm not going to let you leave me in this moment."

As I pulled in a deep breath, a tear escaped my eye. He kissed it away before kissing my lips.

"It's okay," he muttered against my lips before inhaling a shaky breath of his own. "I got you, bae."

Between his sexy voice, the sound of his pleasure, and how good he felt inside of me, I couldn't take anymore. Our eyes locked briefly, just long enough for me to tell him I trusted him with me before I was cumming again... and again... and again.

I WAS SO LOST IN MY THOUGHTS I DIDN'T REALIZE I wasn't alone until Beethoven refilled my glass. Quickly wiping away my tears, I gave him a soft smile.

"You wanna talk about it?" he asked.

I appreciated the fact that he asked instead of assuming that just because I was clearly sad I wanted to talk.

After we went several rounds, I figured I'd be out for the night. That hadn't been the case. I woke up around three in the morning missing my parents, especially Robert Carter, like crazy. His absence in my life was fresher than Mama's.

Being with Beethoven was bittersweet. I loved being with a man who took care of me and made me feel safe like my father, but at times, it made me miss him even more.

And knowing I wouldn't have Beethoven forever made the low moments feel worse. He was going to be another person to leave me, and I was dreading that already.

I wanted to blame the sex and say it was so good it had me open, and maybe that was the case a little, but more than that—this was a heart issue—a heart issue that I had no clue how to fix.

"I miss my daddy," I confessed quietly, wiping away a tear. "And my mama." Chuckling, I sniffled. "And I'm already missing you too."

He sat behind me on the window bench. Instead of replying right away, Beethoven wrapped me in his arms and looked out at the moon with me. The soft kiss he placed on my neck soothed me, allowing me to melt against his frame.

"I heard this Memphis author say grief is just leftover love. Love you can't give to someone physically in that moment you miss and want them most." My eyes closed as I buried his words in my mind and heart. "There's nothing wrong with being sad, but instead, I think you should be grateful. Grateful that you had two loving parents for as long as you did. Grateful that you're capable of loving them beyond the grave. I know nothing or no one can take their place, but I'm here, and I'll hold the space for them—and that love. And I can love on you too." As I wiped away more tears, I looked back at him. "And as far as you missing me... bae, I'm not leaving you no time soon. I don't have to leave you ever."

"But you said you wanted to leave Memphis."

"That doesn't mean we can't stay in touch. Besides, that won't happen any time soon. If you focus on the past, you'll be sad and depressed. If you focus on the future, you'll be anxious and worried. All we have is right now, this very moment. And in this very moment, I got you."

That was true, so I accepted it. Snuggling deeper against his chest, I pulled in a deep breath and tried to focus on this moment. This moment where I had him and I had others to love and be loved by, and I prayed that God would grace me to allow that to be enough.

Beethoven

The Next Morning

AT FIRST, I THOUGHT I WAS HEARING THINGS. THERE was no reason for anyone to be at my door before I woke up. Whiskee stirred against me, pressing her thick ass against my dick.

"Baby, get the door." Her groggy voice was sexy as hell. I didn't think there was anything about this woman I wouldn't find attractive.

My eyes slowly opened and looked out of the window. It looked like the sun hadn't been too long started to rise. Grabbing my phone, I ignored the doorbell and looked at my security camera. At the sight of my father, I groaned. If he was here this early in the morning, it wasn't for something good. After rubbing and squeezing Whiskee's ass and giving her a kiss on the side of her mouth, I got out of bed to see what this man wanted.

"Aight, aight, I'm coming!" I yelled when he continued to ring the doorbell, as if he could hear me.

The shit was so incessant I was annoyed by the time I made it to the front door and swung it open. My frown slowly relaxed when he extended a cup of coffee in my direction.

"I know it's early, but I wanted to see you before my flight."

"Where you goin'?" I asked, accepting the coffee.

"New York. Might have a new connect out that way."

My head bobbed as I sipped the coffee. "How long you gon' be gone, and who going witchu?"

"Just today. I'll be back tomorrow. And I'm taking Denim and two guards."

"Cool."

He loosened his tie, looking past me into the house. "Whiskee here?"

I wasn't sure why he was asking me that. He'd never asked before. Motioning for him to step back, I stepped onto the porch and closed the door behind me.

"Why do you ask?"

"I just wanna make sure you don't blur the lines too much and forget the whole point of this. It's in your best interest if you don't get attached to the girl."

"Like you made sure you didn't get attached to my mama?" His eyes rolled toward the sky. I didn't bother to give him time to respond. It didn't matter anyway. "Not that it's any of your business, but what makes you think I have?"

"Carlos called me last night and told me things were real between you two."

I chuckled as I took a sip of my coffee.

This nigga.

"What me and Whiskee do ain't got shit to do with

either one of y'all. I'on know why he even called to tell you that."

Pops sucked his teeth, ignoring my frustration like he normally did. "I think he did it because he thought it would gain him some brownie points. Regardless, you need to slow down with that. How you think she gon' feel when you kill her brother? That's the whole point of this, son."

"Nah, the point of this was to bring them into the family by marriage, and that's what we're doing."

"I told you in order for this to work, you'd have to kill him and take over."

"No, you said in order for this to work, I had to marry her. You said you wanted him dead, and that was only if we felt like he couldn't handle business. I never agreed to that, just to marrying her to bring them in."

He chuckled before drinking his coffee. "There you go again... saying things that suggest you think you have a choice." His smile dropped. "I'm not asking you anything; I'm telling you that you're going to kill him. Now if you can lay next to her knowing you killed her brother, go forth. If not, cut all this lovey dovey shit out and focus on the business." As he turned, he added, "I'll call you when I get back home."

There was no point in me trying to go back and forth with him, so as frustrated as I was, I went back inside and finished my coffee before brushing my teeth and handling my hygiene in the guest bathroom that was nearest the kitchen.

Whiskee was in the gym working out, which didn't surprise me. Every step that I took toward her made my heart ache more and more. I didn't want to be the reason she lost another person that was close to her. If something happened to Carlos, she'd feel alone in this world. I didn't know how I was going to make this work for all of us, but I'd have to figure something out—soon.

After our workout, we showered together, then got back in bed. I wasn't used to this slow way of living, but I could appreciate the rest. She had a specific post-workout smoothie that she wanted, so I ordered us two. I didn't realize how quiet I'd been until she called me out on it and asked me was I okay.

"Yeah, just got some shit on my mind."

"Does it have to do with that early visit?"

Nodding, I wrapped my arm around her shoulders and pulled her closer to me in the center of my king-sized bed. Resting my back on the headboard, I told her, "It does, but that's not something for you to worry about. I'll figure it out."

She gave me a smile that melted my heart as she cupped my cheek and stroked it with her thumb. "I'm sure you will."

As long as we got it in last night, I would think we both had enough. But realistically, I didn't think I'd ever get enough of Whiskee, and as our lips connected, I was glad she was on the same page. Kisses and touches led to her straddling me and pulling my dick out of my boxers.

As she bounced up and down on my dick, I feasted on her neck and nipples. The wetter she got, the harder it was for me to maintain control. And when her bounces hardened and the sound of her ass smacking against me filled the room, that shit damn near made me lose my mind.

While she rocked against me, I squeezed and rubbed her ass.

That first quake shook her, signaling she'd be cumming soon.

I didn't want to think about how good she rode dick.

Or how many men had felt this pleasure before.

How many men would feel it after me.

That would make me far too possessive of her.

Instead, I forced myself to remain in this present moment and enjoy every day with Whiskee that I had.

Beethoven

Late April

WHAT WAS SUPPOSED TO BE A CELEBRATORY DINNER was about to be over before it could start. When I left Memphis, I was under the impression Whiskee would be with her brother while I was gone. Mahogany had a brand trip to take. At the last minute, Pops asked Carlos to go with him to Miami, and the dumb ass agreed. As furious as I was, I was trying to keep calm. Ike was big on professionalism, and I didn't want to curse Carlos's ass out while I was in his home.

Squeezing the bridge of my nose, I pulled in a deep breath.

"Why would you agree to go on the trip knowing no one would be there for my wife?"

"I didn't think I could tell your pops no. The professional relationship is still new. I didn't want him to think I wasn't reliable."

"So it's more important to you that my father think you're reliable than your sister's emotional well-being?"

Carlos huffed. "Look, can you leave the meeting and go get her or not?"

"I'm not in Memphis, nigga," I seethed quietly, feeling like I was about to explode. "It's gonna take me three damn hours to get back home. By then, it'll be well after midnight."

"Shit. Okay. Let me see if one of my homies can go and at least sit outside of their apartment. That's going to have to do until you can get there. Damn. Had I known your meeting wasn't in Memphis, I would have told him no."

This conversation was useless to me, so I ended the call. Dialing Mama's number, I shot Omari a look before leaving the dining room. It was important to me that we made a great impression with Ike tonight, but nothing was more important to me right now than Whiskee's mental state.

"Hey, baby," Mama answered with a smile in her voice. "How's your trip going?"

"Well, thank you. Listen, I need a favor."

"Anything."

"Whiskee is at home by herself for the first time in years. She... has a thing about being alone at night, and I won't be back for several hours."

"Will she be comfortable with me?"

"I'm sure she will be. I'm gonna call her and see if she wants you there until me or her best friend can get to her. If so, can you go pick her up?"

"Of course, baby. Just keep me posted."

Relief filled me as I thanked her and ended the call, then called Whiskee. It took forever for her to answer, and when she did, I heard the deep, shaky breath she took.

"H-hey, baby." She sniffled, and the sound was like a punch to my gut. "How did it go?"

"Fuck this. How are you?"

Whiskee cleared her throat. "I'm fine, Beethoven."

"Don't lie to me. I'm 'bout to send you a FaceTime request."

"No, don't!" she yelled softly, quickly. "I'm scared, I'm not gonna lie, but I'll be okay."

"I'm sorry, bae. If I would've known your brother was leaving, I would've brought you with me."

Whiskee chuckled, but it turned into another sniffle. "I can't suffer with this forever, right?"

"Bae... I need to see you to know you're okay. Can I please FaceTime you?"

She thought about it for a while before agreeing. When the FaceTime connected and I saw her red, puffy eyes, my heart broke into pieces. She was sitting against the wall with her knees to her chest. On the nightstand next to her was the 9mm that was supposed to be inside of it for emergencies.

"You remember we put bars on the windows, right?" She nodded, tugging her bottom lip into her mouth as her chin trembled and eyes watered. "And the door is an armored door now, bae. No one can get in. You're *so* safe, Whiskee, I promise."

Her head nodded rapidly and eyes squeezed shut. "Okay," she whispered.

"My mama is gonna come and get you, aight? She's going to take you to her home, which is just as secure, and I'll pick you up in a few hours."

She looked into my eyes. "I really appreciate that, but I think I need to be alone. If I don't, I'll never get over this.

You're right; I'm safe here. I'm uncomfortable and scared, but I'll make it through the night."

"Are you absolutely sure, because she's ready to come if she needs to."

Whiskee took a deep breath and nodded. "I'm sure, baby. Thank you. Besides, I don't want the first time we meet to be while I'm on my bullshit."

Her smile made me smile. "My mama don't care about that kind of stuff. She knows I care about you, so she cares about you too. If you need her to come, she'll be there."

"Okay. I'll keep that in mind, but I really think I'll be okay."

"Aight. I'll send you her number just in case. If you need her before I get there, just call her."

"Okay, baby. I will."

We talked for a few seconds more before ending the call. I sent her Mama's contact card, and she saved her number before I went back into the dining room. Though, being honest, the last thing I wanted to do at that moment was eat, drink, and be merry. I wanted to get to my wife. She was right, though. Maybe her being alone tonight was for the best. I just hated that she didn't have time to mentally prepare for it. Hopefully, she'd be okay. If she wasn't, Mama would pull up on her, and I'd be right behind her.

Whiskee

Trying to sleep made the fear worse. As long as I was up and alert, I was scared but okay. When I tried to sleep, that was when the nightmares started. All I could see was my mother tied up and telling me she loved me before a bullet entered her head. Around midnight, I gave up the fight to sleep. My phone vibrated, and the text from Beethoven's mom made me smile.

Lisa: Hey baby. It's Lisa... Bay's mama. I just wanted to check on you.

Hi. I'm hanging in here. I don't think I'll get to sleep any time soon, so I'm about to make some tea and try to do something productive.

Lisa: Well I'm parked outside if you need me.

No ma'am! I didn't know you were here. Come on up!

Lisa: Are you sure?

I'm positive.

A couple of minutes later, there was a knock on the door. I looked through the peephole and let her in.

"Hello," she greeted, stepping inside.

"Hey, I'm so sorry you've been sitting out there. Hopefully, you weren't out there for too long."

"Just a couple of hours. Bay told me you'd call if you needed me, but I was too worried to wait."

I wasn't sure why, but her concern warmed me and made me reach for a hug. Maybe it was because I hadn't had a nurturing, motherly figure in so many years. Either way, I appreciated her concern.

She gave me a warm, lingering hug that brought tears to my eyes, but I was able to compose myself.

"Thank you for coming," I muttered as I released her.

"You're welcome, and I'm like Disney. I'll never end a hug until you do."

"Good to know," I said through my laugh.

We went into the kitchen, where I fixed us both a cup of tea. I'd baked a sweet potato pie for dessert two nights ago, so I cut us both a piece of that as well. Lisa kind of looked like Beethoven, but he definitely looked more like his daddy. He got his eye color and lip shape from her, but everything else about his features came from Tim.

"How have things been with you and my Bay?" she broke the silence to ask while we sat at the island.

"Great," I cooed with a smile that made her giggle like a schoolgirl. "I never thought being betrayed and forced into an arranged marriage could lead to me meeting such an amazing man, but it has. I really, really like him."

"Did he tell you his father and I had an arranged marriage too? Only I wasn't so lucky."

"He told me briefly. It seemed to be a difficult subject for him to talk about, so he didn't share much."

"I'm not surprised. I didn't tell him about it until he told me about you."

"Oh, wow. Is there a reason you kept it a secret?"

She thought about it briefly, wrapping her hands around her mug. "I didn't want it to change the way he viewed either of us. It was my plan to tell him when he was an adult and capable of understanding. But when he turned eighteen, I decided to leave Tim and it didn't matter anymore."

"Well, at least you're free now. I haven't been around Tim a lot, but I definitely don't see him winning any father-in-law of the year awards with me."

That good a hearty laugh out of her, which made me smile. We continued to talk and drink and eat... well into the morning. From relationships to spirituality to woman-hood and needless gossip, we talked about it all. I didn't think we started to get tired until after two in the morning. At that point, I showed her where the empty guest bedroom was so she could rest. When I made it to my room, I brushed my teeth and washed my face then texted my man.

Thank you baby. Your mom is great. I love her.

Mr. Smith: Y'all funny. She just texted me that you're the best and she loves you 😂

I hearted the message and yawned before drifting off into a peaceful sleep, grateful not just for Beethoven but for Lisa too.

B. Love

Some Hours Later...

At the feel of the bed denting, I shifted. With a shriek, I was about to hop out of bed until Beethoven said, "Shh... it's just me."

Relaxing in his arms, I settled onto his chest. "What time is it?"

"A little after five. I would've gotten here sooner but Ike invited some of his associates over and that shit turned into a whole party. Any other time that would have been cool, but I was anxious to get back to you."

Tossing my leg over him, I kissed his chest. "I'm good, baby. You didn't have to rush back home for me. I did have a low moment, but your mom texted me at the perfect time. I didn't even know she was sitting out there."

"Yeah, I told her she didn't have to, but she never listens to me."

Chuckling softly, I looked up at him, though I could barely see him in the darkness. The only light I had was the moonlight shining through the windows.

"You really care about me... don't you?"

"More than I thought was possible."

"Thank you."

Beethoven gave me a soft, sweet kiss. "You don't have to thank me for that, bae."

"Yes, I do. You're not required to care about me or treat me well."

"I am, actually. If for nothing else but on a spiritual level, it's my responsibility to treat you well. If I don't, I'll suffer. You're a gift from God to me. I'm going to cherish you for as long as you'll allow."

Our kiss was slow, tender... hungry. Beethoven rolled me over, and as much as I wanted him inside me, I said, "Baby... your mama is here."

Sucking his teeth, Beethoven pulled my satin gown over my head. "She sleep, and even if she ain't, we grown."

"Beetho—ah..."

The warmth of his mouth on my nipple silenced any reservations I had. And when his hand slipped between my thighs, I was completely under his spell.

"You're a very bad influence." I giggled, but it turned into a moan when his middle finger entered me.

"You like this shit though."

"I love it."

Beethoven's mouth latched around my clit, and I held my legs open as he feasted on me. When I felt myself about to cum and get loud, I pushed him away. His protests stopped quickly when I rolled him over and took his shaft into my mouth. I'd been aching to taste him, and it was very much worth the wait. He was so long and thick, I could barely take all of him down my throat. My gagging turned him on. He pulled my bonnet off and palmed my hair, moaning as I slobbered and sucked him in deeper.

The shaky breaths he released made me moan as my pussy leaked. When he began to roll his hips and fuck my face, I could no longer resist fingering my pussy until I came. Quiet whimpers escaped me and combined with the sound of him moaning my name.

When he couldn't take it anymore, Beethoven pulled me up and placed me on my side. He slid into me from behind, filling me with swift, hard strokes that had me moaning his name and whimpering until we both crashed and fell asleep.

Beethoven

"I want grandbabies, but I don't want to hear you making 'em."

My mother's declaration caused me to choke on the orange juice I was drinking. Whiskee made us breakfast, and I was glad she was in the bathroom; otherwise, she would have been embarrassed.

"Really, Ma?"

"Don't *really Ma* me. You knew I was here."

"Yeah, but I thought you was sleep. Plus... I didn't too much care. I wasn't expecting you to say anything about it, though."

Chuckling, she swatted my arm as she stood. "Come walk me to the door, boy."

"Aight."

They'd said their goodbyes before Whiskee left, and now I saw why her messy ass hung around to say that silly shit. That was my mama, though, and I loved her.

"You take care of my daughter-in-law," she ordered before giving me a hug and kiss on the cheek.

"Yes, ma'am. Thank you again for pulling up. She might not have said it, but she needed that."

"I could tell. We talked a little about her mom and it broke my heart to know someone could be so evil not just to kill her but in front of her daughter."

Looking back toward the hall, I considered if I wanted to tell her the truth. "How about your ex-husband knew and didn't do shit about it?" I whispered.

Her eyes widened and she gripped my arm. "*What?*"

"Yeah. Apparently, Uncle Mario wanted to put her father out of commission for a while, so Malik was supposed to rob and attack him. Robert and her brother weren't at home, so Malik robbed them and killed her mama."

"Oh my God," Mama whispered, cupping her cheek. "Does she know your cousin..."

My head shook as I looked down the hall again. "Nah. Do you think I should tell her?"

"Let me ask you this." She paused and pulled in a deep breath. "Are you the reason Mario is in a wheelchair and Malik is still in a coma?" I nodded. "This is tough, son. You didn't know and when you found out, you handled them. I don't know, baby. She might resent you for what they did. It would be different if there was a chance she never had to come in contact with them, but seeing as they are your family, that could be tricky. With that in mind, if they ever were to be around her and let it slip out what they did and that you knew, that could blow up in your face too. I think you should find a way to see if she wants to know who was responsible. If not, I wouldn't tell her. It's a shame they're family; otherwise, I would have said kill them both."

"Family or not, I wanted to kill them. Pops told me not to."

"This is exactly why I hate this business. There's no

reason you should have to carry a weight like this. I'll be praying it works in your favor and that it will never be an issue for the two of you."

"Thank you, Ma. I 'preciate you."

I walked her to her car, and we said our goodbyes before I went back into the apartment, where I gave Whiskee a full update on the meeting yesterday. Neither I nor Omari wanted to sell weed to users. We were beyond that. I was more interested in the concept of exporting across the country, however, that would create more risks. We did put on the table opening and operating legal dispensaries, which I hadn't considered before. The streets and being a drug dealer was all I knew. Even when it came to our legal businesses, we had managers and assistants that handled all that.

If we were to export product for legal dispensaries, that would take a hell of a lot of the risks out, and legal weed was a billion-dollar industry. Exporting to legal dispensaries would also provide the legacy and security I'd want for my children and their children. It would also allow me to be with a woman who wasn't in this lifestyle and not have to worry about her safety. That was a big concern that had been weighing on me after hearing about what happened to Renee and seeing how it affected Whiskee. I never wanted something I did to be the reason someone else suffered or died, especially my wife and kids.

With Whiskee in my life, my perspective had been changing when it came down to a lot of things. While a part of me hoped she could be by my side to reap the benefits, I also understood how attached she was to her brother. Even with their relationship hitting a rocky patch, I didn't see her leaving him... even if it was to go to Rose Valley Hills with me.

That Weekend

WHISKEE AND MAHOGANY HIGH WAS A TRIP. THEY wanted to celebrate Mahogany landing a huge brand deal and I offered to throw a lil set at my place. Of course I invited my crew and between the liquor flowing and weed, practically everyone was cross faded. With all the food we had, their high asses wanted pizza from Little Caesar's of all places. But whatever my baby wanted... my baby got. I felt like a daddy buying pizza for his kid's class when I pulled back up with ten boxes of pizza, but their happiness made it worth it.

Now, they were cackling and gossiping out by the pool with the rest of the women while the guys and I chilled in my game room. I even sent an invite to her brother, though I didn't care if he came or not. It was my way of trying to develop some kind of relationship with him. If I was going to be able to spare his life, he would have to prove he was valuable to Pops. So all night, I picked at his brain to see if he had any qualities that I could amplify. Being the boss of all bosses wouldn't be a good fit, but from the sound of it, he didn't have a problem bussing a gun and he was good at keeping up with product and numbers.

"If you could choose what you did in the business, what would it be?" I asked, handing him another beer.

"Shit, I'on know, Bay. I never wanted to be in charge, though Pops always told me it would be a possibility. The only other man he trusted to take over died two years before him, and he never prioritized training someone else to take his place. I guess I'd want to do something I could truly be successful at."

"And what has that been in the past?"

"I'm good in any role when it comes down to production. Breaking it down, weighing it, packing it up, dividing it. I was great at staying on top of our lieutenants and making sure nobody came up short. Before we got two new accountants, I was his money man. That was a more difficult responsibility to have with more pressure, but I was good at that too."

I thought about it for a while before asking him to follow me onto the veranda. After sparking up a blunt I told him, "What if there was a way you could be over production but nothing else? Your father's organization would stay in business, my pops would remain your supplier, but there would be a different boss of all bosses."

"Who would it be? You?"

"Maybe, maybe not. If not me, my pops." I didn't want to give him any information about my plan. He'd proven he couldn't be trusted once, and I wouldn't make that mistake again. If I went the legal route, I wouldn't be involved in Pops' organization or Carlos's new position. If I didn't, I'd take over. Either way, Pops would have the control he wanted, and I could spare Carlos's life and Whiskee's heart in the process.

"I'on know how I feel about giving over complete control of my father's organization to someone else; however, I can admit I'm not the best fit. I would thrive more if I was over production and production alone. Let me think on it, aight?"

That was good enough for me. As Pops would say—I'd let him think about it, but he really didn't have a choice. It was either he stand down and handle production or Pops would have him killed, whether I did it or not.

Whiskee

T he Following Tuesday

Today, Mariam set up taste tests for me and Beethoven. It was overwhelming to say the least. Not just because we had a lot to try but because we had to make our decisions today as well. The wedding was exactly two months away and finalizing the menu was the last thing on our to-do list. We'd already selected the music and officiant, venue, décor and color scheme, stationery for invitations, and thank-you cards.

After this, we'd have to meet with the designer to go over the sketch and my measurements for the dress, then that would be it. Beethoven and I agreed not to bother with bachelor and bachelorette parties, but we did agree to an engagement party so his family could be in attendance. The good thing about this process was our bond and chemistry were genuine, so no one should question our feelings for each other.

With the bulk of the planning being done, Tim wanted Beethoven to get back to work, so we hadn't been spending as much time together as we had been. That made me grateful for the meeting with Mariam today. I was even more grateful when Beethoven asked me if I wanted to do a late lunch.

We decided on The Capital Grille, and as we sat across from each other, I was nervous. I knew this was the same man I'd been getting to know for the last month and a half, but it felt new.

"Why you actin' shy?" Beethoven asked as he looked over the menu.

"I don't know." With a quiet laugh, I twiddled my thumbs in my lap. "I feel like I haven't seen you in forever, but it's only been like three days. I think I missed my husband."

His grip on the menu loosened as he stared at me. "That's the first time you've called me that."

"Really?"

"Yeah, really."

"Hmm..."

"If that's what I get from being less present, maybe I need to work more."

That made me laugh. "Well, I'll never stop a man from working, but I really did miss you, Beethoven."

"I missed you too. Tryna balance Pops business on top of what me and Omari are trying to do in Rose Valley Hills is a lot."

"I understand. Is there anything I can do to help?"

"You can convince your brother to stand down and be the head of production only."

Our waiter arrived, taking our drink and appetizer

order. When he left, I asked, "Is there a particular reason why Carlos needs a different position?"

"Yeah. He's not built to be the boss. Not right now at least." He paused and inhaled a long breath. "On top of that... it's safer for him if he does something else."

"What do you mean? He's aware of the risks of being the boss, Beethoven."

"Nah." His head shook as he picked his menu back up. "I'm not talking about enemies and law enforcement. There's a very present threat looming that he has no idea about. The only way to get rid of it is for him to stand down."

I didn't respond as I thought over what he said. I wasn't the smartest when it came down to their affairs, but I also wasn't dumb. If someone was going to come after my brother because of his position, it had to be Tim.

"Is it your father? Is he not pleased with what my brother is doing?"

Beethoven sighed as he put his menu back down. "Yeah, and it's not that he's not pleased, though he isn't. Business is business, and with the amount of product and money that flows from us to y'all, Pops can't take any risks with a weak boss. Your brother can't handle his emotions, he makes illogical decisions, and he doesn't have enough experience to head an organization of this size. Now, I'm not saying he's not going to be a good boss one day, but he's simply not ready right now."

"So Tim wants my father's business? Has that been his plan all along? He never wanted to work with us. He's always wanted to take over. Hasn't he?"

"I'd prefer not to discuss this with you. I just need you to talk to your brother and convince him to stand down."

"What was your part in this?" I asked, ignoring what

he'd just said. "To get close to me so I could convince him to give y'all the business?"

Beethoven massaged the space between his eyes and stared at me. "Are we about to have our first disagreement?"

"It doesn't have to be. Just tell me the truth."

"No, it was not my job to get close to you so you could influence him. I was supposed to marry you to bring the both of you into the family. That's it."

"If he doesn't agree, then what?" He didn't respond right away, and the longer he remained silent, the more my heart palpitated. "Bay..."

"If he doesn't agree, he dies."

"And let me guess... you're the one that's supposed to kill him?" Chuckling, I stood. "I'm going home."

Beethoven stood. "Whiskee..."

"I'm going to Uber. I don't want to be around you."

Before I could walk away, he gripped my waist. "We need to talk about this."

"There's nothing to talk about. You've known all along your father wanted you to kill my brother and you've allowed me to get close to you." Shoving his hand from my waist, I gritted, "That's *sick*."

I got a couple of steps in, but he grabbed my hand and pulled me back, causing eyes and heads to turn in our direction.

"I've been trying to find a way to keep him alive. This is the only chance he has, bae. Get him to stand down and he won't have to worry about me or anyone else from the organization coming after him."

Jerking away from him, I hurried out of the dining area and hoped he wouldn't follow me. Here I was looking forward to marrying this man, even if it wouldn't last forever, and he'd been plotting to kill my brother the whole damn time.

"WELL, AT LEAST HE WAS HONEST," MAHOGANY muttered.

"I wish he would have lied."

Pouting, I swirled the glass of wine I'd been babysitting for the last hour as we talked.

"Aww, you don't mean that."

"I actually do. He ruined the fairytale I'd been in. Now that I know the truth, there's no way I can be with him."

"I don't know about that, sis. I mean... I could see if he didn't tell you and tried to kill your brother, but he was honest and he said he's been trying to find a way to keep Los alive. That has to count for something... right?" When I didn't answer, she continued, "I think you should talk to Carlos. Convince him to stand down. If Tim wants to be in control, from what you've told me about him, nothing will stop him. I don't think you want to make an enemy out of Bay. I think you should try and keep him on your side."

"See that's just the thing. A part of me knows Beethoven would never let anything happen to me, and I think he includes my brother in that because he's an extension of me."

"Then what's the real issue here, Whiskee?"

Setting my wine glass on the island, I thought over how honest I wanted to be with my best friend, only because I hadn't been fully honest with myself.

"What if this is a sign that I need to start detaching from him? We won't be together forever anyway. Even if Carlos does stand down, Beethoven will be leaving soon. Maybe

138

it's for the best if I stop getting attached to him now. Make it easier on myself."

"Except you're already falling in love with him, babes."

There it was... the truth I'd been wanting to avoid.

I should have known I wouldn't be able to avoid it with her.

Gulping down my wine, I stared at the ceiling as she laughed at my expense and gave me a hug.

"Admit it, Whis. You're falling hard for that man, and that's okay. I got a feeling Beethoven is strong enough to catch you."

The doorbell rang, and I shot up to answer the door, grateful for a distraction. What I wasn't grateful for, or maybe I was, was the sight of Beethoven. Those golden-brown eyes... those juicy lips. God. This man was too hand-some for his own good.

"Huh." He extended a bag in my direction, and when I noticed it was full of my favorite snacks I laughed. "Figured you'd appreciate that more than flowers."

"I do, but what are you doing here? I told you I didn't want to be around you."

"Still?" Between the confusion on his face and distress in his voice, he was making it harder and harder to want to stay away from him. Sucking his teeth, Beethoven crossed his arms over his chest. "For how long?"

"I don't know, baby. It's only been a few hours. I don't know how long it takes to get over your man plotting to kill your brother."

"I wasn't..." With a groan, he covered his face as his head shook. "I don't regret being honest with you, but I wish I wouldn't have told you today. I wish I would have waited until your brother agreed to stand down so we could have avoided this."

He lowered his hands and looked into my eyes.

"Honestly, Beethoven, I don't think it would have made a difference. My brother is the only family I have left. Your father wanting to bring him harm will never be okay. I do respect and appreciate you trying to find a way to spare him, and I will talk to Carlos about standing down. I guess his decision will determine if I will feel comfortable enough being with you."

"I can accept that. Regardless of what happens between us personally, though, the wedding still has to happen, or this conversation won't matter." He placed a kiss to the center of my forehead. "I'll see you in a couple of days for the meeting with Mariam."

"Okay."

As much as I wanted him to stay, I was glad Beethoven left without putting up a fight. Getting him out of my system would be torture. God... I prayed somehow that I didn't have to.

Beethoven

It kind of worked out that Whiskee drove herself to the meeting with Mariam because I was late. When I arrived, I went straight to where they told me Whiskee was. It didn't register in my brain that I was going into a fitting room. Not until I pulled the curtain back and saw her in a beautiful white gown that took my breath away. It was silk, which she'd told me was her favorite fabric. The spaghetti straps drew my attention to collarbones I hadn't been able to kiss in what felt like an eternity.

The flowy design hugged her where it should and was loose where needed, puddling at her feet.

"Wow," I mumbled. "You look..." My head shook as I took small steps toward her. "Absolutely stunning, bae. You're going to make such a beautiful bride."

"Thank you." She released a nervous chuckle as she turned and looked from herself to me behind her in the mirror. "It's a good thing I passed on this one since you've seen me in it. Though I guess it doesn't matter since it's not a real wedding anyway. Well, it's a real wedding. Just not a real marriage." Whiskee huffed and smoothed the fabric against her skin. "I think I want something more... fancy. This seems too basic. Maybe I could wear this for the engagement party. What do you think?"

"That sounds perfect to me."

Unable to resist, I wrapped my arms around her and kissed her neck, grateful she didn't push me away. In fact, she melted against me.

"Baby," she called softly, biting down on her bottom lip as she smiled.

"I miss my wife."

Her eyes fluttered and closed as she turned in my embrace. "Your wife misses you too."

I used my nose against hers to tilt her head back before kissing her deeply. My hands lowered to her ass, and the only reason I didn't lift her into the air and slide her down on my dick was because I knew someone could walk behind this curtain just as easily as I had.

"What are we going to do?" she asked against my lips.

"We're not going to do anything. Your brother is going to stand down, and we won't have an issue anymore."

"Still, Bay." Her hands slid down my chest. "You're going to be leaving me soon. Do you really think it's wise for us to get even closer than we are now?"

Chuckling, I took her hands into mine and kissed them. "It's a little too late to be thinking about that, Whiskee. I'm falling in love with you."

Her mouth dropped as Mariam said, "Are you sure he came this way? I don't see him."

After giving her a quick kiss, I told her, "Let me get out here before she thinks we're being nasty."

Whiskee swallowed hard as she stared at me. Snapping out of her trance, she nodded as her mouth closed. I made my way back outside to the sitting area as Mariam walked through it again. Relief covered her face at the sight of me.

"There you are! I was worried you wouldn't be able to make it. Your tuxedos are behind curtain number three."

Following her guidance, I went to my fitting room and tried on three tuxedos that looked pretty much the same, just with small differences. By the time I was done, Whiskee was dressed and talking to the designer about some changes to her wedding dress. When we were done, I asked her if I could walk her to her car and she said yes.

"What you about to get into?" I asked.

"Mahogany and Carlos wanted to take me out tonight to celebrate me getting my cosmetology license renewed."

Pride swelled within my heart as I pulled her into my arms. "Word, bae? That's amazing. Congratulations. I'm so fucking proud of you."

"Thank you so much. I feel good about it. I'm happy."

"Good, you deserve it."

Licking my lips, I looked down at her and resisted the urge to kiss her.

"You're more than welcome to join us if you'd like."

"I'd be honored."

Releasing her, I opened the door to her red Porsche as she told me where they'd be and what time. Just before I was about to close the door, she said, "Oh, Beethoven?"

"Yeah?"

"I'm falling in love with you too."

Her giggle was like music to my ears as she closed the door since I was just holding it. Whatever it took, I'd have to get this woman in Rose Valley Hills with me.

"Baby, you didn't have to do all this."

Whiskee wiped a few tears as she looked over everything I'd gotten her. We'd come back to my place after her celebratory dinner. To congratulate her, I'd gotten her a few pieces of fine jewelry from Elite's jewelry store that she'd been gushing over all night, along with six figures in cash and the email confirmation for her appointment with Cooper—who had my permission to show her whatever buildings she wanted for her salon.

"You deserve this and more. I really am proud of you for doing something for yourself. It takes courage to get back out there, and I got you every step of the way."

Her countenance fell, and I didn't like how every time we were together now it seemed like something was on her mind and heart. Wanting to ease that load I asked, "What's on your mind?"

Looking away, Whiskee nibbled her cheek. "Just... thinking about how much I'm going to miss you when you leave."

Gently, I sat her on the bench next to the gifts and lowered myself to take off her heels. "What if you don't have to miss me?"

"You're not leaving anymore?"

"I am... but what if you come with me?"

I stood and lifted her, then lifted her dress over her head. As much as I wanted to take her panties and bra off and feast on her pussy, it was important to me that we had this conversation. I allowed her to keep her underwear on, then put her in the center of my bed.

"You want me to move there with you?"

Chuckling, I nodded. "Isn't that what I just said?"

"Well, yes, but I wanted to make sure you knew that."

Another laugh escaped me before I gave her a soft kiss.

"I know what I said, and that's exactly what I meant." Taking her hand into mine, I kissed each of her knuckles. "I was thinking the marriage could be real too. For your brother, we'll keep things planned for June. For ourselves, we'll date and continue to get to know each other and adjust to life and our partnership, and when we're ready, we can renew our vows and do another wedding—with pure intentions that time."

"Wait." Her smile was wide as she sat up on her elbow and looked down at me. "You're saying you want to marry me for real?"

"Yeah. I don't want to let you go, Whiskee. And maybe that's selfish of me bu—"

My words were replaced with a moan because of our kiss. Even if she didn't say vocally that she was pleased with what I said, she showed me by sucking the soul out of my dick and taking back shots that had her cum cascading down it.

Whiskee

T he Next Morning

SINCE LAST NIGHT, I HADN'T BEEN ABLE TO STOP smiling. Knowing that Beethoven wanted to marry me for real had me on a cloud. We agreed to date for a year while married, and if we still wanted to be together, our vow renewal would be the start of our real marriage. It was backward as hell, but it worked for us. If we did it this way, not only would Carlos be safe and Robert Carter's organization would still have its supplier, but I'd have my man and we'd be able to live our lives happily and legally in Rose Valley Hills.

The only downside to moving was leaving my brother and best friend. Just the thought was able to wipe my smile away. I would be okay without Carlos because he'd been working like crazy, but my sisterhood with Mahogany was on a deeper level. She was truly my soulmate, and regardless of how good things were going with Beethoven, I didn't want to lose my girl.

I made my way into her room and crawled into bed with her. It was a rare occasion where she didn't have to go live or post any videos, and she planned to spend the day catching up on movies and shows. Outside of going to look at a few buildings with Cooper, I didn't have anything else planned, so I told her I'd watch a few things with her this evening.

"I'm sad," I muttered, causing her to look over at me with a smile.

"Why?"

"Beethoven wants to be with me for real for real. He wants me to move to Rose Valley Hills with him."

Her smile widened as she sat up in bed and I did the same. "That's amazing, Whiskee! Why on earth would you be sad about that?"

"I don't want to leave you. You've been by my side forever. We see each other literally every day. How am I going to adjust to not having you?"

"Is that all you're worried about?" She laughed. "I'll just move there."

For a while we just stared at each other before bursting into a fit of laughter.

"Don't play with me, Mahogany."

"I'm not! I can do social media literally anywhere. You're my sister and I love you. I don't want to be without you either. It's nothing for me to move. My husband might be there waiting for me, 'cause he for damn sure ain't here."

I hugged her neck tightly, fighting back my tears. "You just made me so, so happy! Oh my God, I love you so much."

I didn't think anything could make the progression of me and Beethoven's relationship better... but having my sister with me in Rose Valley Hills just took the fucking cake.

THE WEEKEND HAD BEEN AMAZING. FRIDAY, Beethoven and I went to a car show, which was super fun. Yesterday, he took me to my first symphony, and it was so beautiful and emotionally moving I cried. Tonight, I wanted to put together a date for him. He'd been really good to me, and I wanted to do something to show him how much I appreciated him.

During one of our get-to-know-you conversations, he shared that no woman had ever took him on a date and that he'd never ridden in a limo before. He was always the one doing romantic gestures and being sentimental, which was often the case with men. So tonight, I hired a driver and reserved a limo for four hours. We went to the spa for massages and facials, grabbed some drinks and went dancing, then had a romantic dinner and boat ride on the Mississippi River.

After we settled into the limo and prepared to go back to his home, Beethoven said, "No one has ever done anything like this for me. The evening was perfect, bae. Thank you."

"It was my honor and pleasure. I want to treat you just as well as you treat me."

Our lips connected for one of the kisses that I'd absolutely become addicted to. His lips lowered to my neck—his hand lowered between my thighs. As I spread them, I was grateful for the privacy of the partition being raised. We were about to add another first to both of our lists—making love in a limo.

Whiskee

O ne Week Later
Early May

FOR THE TWO MEN IN MY LIFE, I PREPARED A southern feast. They broke bread and tolerated each other over a meal of fried chicken, collard greens, macaroni and cheese, yams, and caramel cake for dessert. The meal was silent except when one was saying something to me, but they were at peace, and I accepted that.

When we were done eating, I gave them both a box of cigars and a bottle of The Macallan. As I looked from Carlos to Beethoven, I said, "Robert Carter gave me this whisky when I turned twenty-one. He told me to save it for a special occasion. I want the special occasion to be you two working together and finding a way to get along."

Carlos scoffed, gently pushing the bottle away. He knew the importance of it. He'd seen it on the bar in my room for years. He heard the speech our father gave me on my twenty-first birthday. How he reminded me of my influence as a woman. How unique I was.

Not just because of my name and appearance but because of my heart and character. How I would come in contact with men who would abuse and misuse me—not understand and appreciate or savor my value. How I would be found by a man who would treat me like the strongest and smoothest whisky... valuing me, cherishing me, savoring me, and treating me in such a unique and special way that I'd feel safe pouring into him and trusting he could pour into me. Beethoven was that person for me, and I prayed my brother would understand and respect that.

"He planned to kill me, sis. I'm here, in peace, because of you."

"If I wanted you dead, you would be," Beethoven replied, taking the whisky, and I held my breath.

"And what? You think I'ma ever trust you? Ever feel safe with you? Ever think your intentions with my sister are pure? How am I supposed to know you're not using her to get to me and my father's organization and when the marriage is done you won't hurt her or me?"

Beethoven's head tilted and he released a hard breath. "I proved my loyalty to you by offering you a solution. One that would allow you to not only have a purpose and be successful but keep your life too. If you don't shift into production, there's literally nothing me or Whiskee can do to save you. If I don't kill you for my father, someone else will."

Sitting on the coffee table in front of them, I looked from one to the other, almost pleading with Carlos with my eyes.

"You used to always say how much you loved working

directly with the different strains," I said, "How creative you felt coming up with your own. The only reason Daddy made you stop was because he didn't have the resources then to put behind you or time to wait because his clientele was growing." I placed my hand on his knee. "That's no longer a problem, brother. You can be the head of production, create the strains you love, and flourish in your position. Your life won't be on the line, and I'll get to be with the man I love."

I hadn't admitted that to Beethoven before, so it didn't surprise me when his head whipped in my direction. Thick brows bunched up and his chiseled jaw clenched as he stared at the side of my face.

"You love him?" Carlos asked softly.

Nodding, I blinked back tears and swallowed my emotion.

"Yes," I choked out with a smile. "And I trust him. With me and with you. If Bay says switching positions will keep you safe and you'll no longer be a target, do it, Los. Please."

Our eyes remained locked for a while before Carlos looked over at Beethoven.

"Aight, I'll do it."

A shaky breath released from my lungs as I smiled and hung my head, silently thanking God. If his pride would have kept him from agreeing, I didn't think there would have been anything else I could do. I grabbed two glasses and poured them both two fingers of whisky before leaving and allowing them to talk.

While I waited for them to finish up, I looked at more buildings online for my salon. I was also considering renting a suite in a salon suite. If I did that, I wouldn't have to worry about as much as I would if I opened my own salon. But, if I did open my own salon, I could make space for other stylists to rent booths. I still had time to decide, especially since I would have to look in both Memphis and Rose Valley Hills. Regardless of which route I took, I was excited about doing what I loved on a more consistent basis.

I wasn't sure how much time had passed before Carlos came into my room and told me he was about to head out. I walked him to the door and gave him a hug, asking that he let me know when he made it home.

"You're never coming back, huh?" he asked with a knowing smile. "That's a lot of house to be in without you."

"Well... maybe... one day soon you'll have a wife and babies to fill it up with."

Carlos chuckled as he gave me a kiss on the forehead. "I doubt that'll happen any time soon, sis. I love you."

"I love you too."

After locking up behind him, I chuckled at the sight of Beethoven's naked frame sliding under my covers. The relaxed him with free time was such a stark difference compared to the busy body he was when we first met. I was glad he had time to not only rest but enjoy the fruit of his labor without having to be on call for Tim twenty-four seven.

"Doesn't take you long to get cozy these days," I teased, pulling my loose-fitting midi dress over my head.

"Never when I know I'm about to cuddle witchu. You've officially turned me into a sap."

That got a good laugh out of me as I climbed into bed and onto his chest.

"You're not a sap, baby. Far from that."

A brief beat of silence passed between us before he asked, "Did you mean what you said? That you loved me?"

"I did. I do."

Beethoven tilted my head by my chin. "I love you."

Lowering his lips to mine, Beethoven gave me a kiss that showed me just what his words had said. And there was absolutely no reason for me to doubt him. For the first time since Robert Carter, I felt completely safe with a man... and I prayed to God that safety would never change.

Beethoven

"You sure about this?" Omari asked, smoothing his already wrinkle-free shirt with his hand. We had to meet with the lieutenants, and I decided now was a great time to talk to Pops about Carlos.

"Now is as good of a time as any," I replied, temporarily putting my phone on Do Not Disturb.

"I'on know, cuz. You know Unc better than me, but are you sure if you tell him about Los and this situation at the same time that he won't flip?"

My head shook as I rang the doorbell then used my key to let us in. "Nah. He needs to know about everything at once so he can process it."

Omari nodded his agreement, though there really wasn't anything he could say to change my mind about this. The sooner he knew about the changes with Carlos so he could prepare the better. We had been making a bit of progress personally over the last week. I invited him out with the crew, and he wasn't annoying or an asshole like

154

usual. Whiskee said it was because he wasn't as stressed out, which I could understand.

"Pops!" I yelled, hoping he was in one of the common areas of his home.

"I'm in the kitchen!"

We went inside, and the sight of him making grits and bacon made me smile. Making breakfast was probably the most normal thing my father did over the years. He might not have been the kind of father to keep me focused on school or push sports on me, but he made sure I ate—physically and financially. Back in the day, Pops always made sure I started my day with a large breakfast. And now, any time we had to talk before noon, I could count on him making me breakfast or bringing me coffee if he was stopping by my place.

"You hungry?" he asked, sliding a plate that was covered with bacon in my direction.

"Yeah," I replied, heading over to the sink to wash my hands.

Omari did the same while Pops fixed our plates. He made a quick skillet of eggs and popped some bread into the toaster before putting everything on the table.

A pot of coffee had already been brewed, so I grabbed it along with some mugs and put them on the table. For a brief moment, I appreciated the peace, because I knew he was going to lose his shit when I told him what I had to tell him.

"Is what you're about to tell me going to fuck up my attitude?" he asked before taking a bite of bacon.

"It might. Depends on how prepared you are." He nodded and motioned in my direction for me to continue. "Leonard found bugs in his meetup spot three days ago."

Pops chewing stopped and he stared at me. His head leaned forward, ear turned more in my direction. "Bugs?"

"Yeah. They were under the table and in a lamp. I met with the rest of the lieutenants this morning after making them all do a sweep of their homes, meetup spots, cars, and warehouses."

"Did anyone else find them?"

"Yeah. About four more."

"Shit," he grumbled, wiping his mouth. "It's cool. We know the feds won't come in until they have a solid case. Going forward, no talking in the same place more than once. No talking inside period. Always in public places. Have them create codes for meeting spots when they are setting them up over the phone."

I locked in what he'd said to spread the word around. "Aight. What about production and distribution? Do you want that to temporarily shut down?"

Sitting back in his seat, he exhaled hardly. "Nah, keep it going. I can't afford to pull back. Just make sure none of you or the lieutenants are seen with product. I can risk a few corner boys going to pick up their product, but I can't risk anyone in the family."

The family.

Clearing my throat, I sat up in my seat. "Speaking of family, I have an update on Carlos."

"What is it?"

"He's moving over to production. You'll get what you want—the entire Carter organization under your control... without having to kill him to get it."

As he chewed the eggs in his mouth, he smiled. "This is because of his sister, isn't it?" His eyes shifted over to Omari for confirmation.

"The reasoning behind it doesn't matter," I replied. "You wanted his men and clientele, and you'll have it. So leave Carlos alone."

He didn't respond either way. He continued to eat as if I hadn't said anything. After I finished my plate, I stood and washed it so I could leave. I didn't believe there was any reason for him to have a personal vendetta against Carlos, so I could only assume he'd let him live. Still, I had to ask, "Are you going to let him live?"

Pops tossed his napkin onto his empty plate and sat back in his seat.

"I don't know," he admitted honestly, which I appreciated. "You getting him out of that role is a premature solution to the problem that has been there from the beginning. Even if Carlos is not the boss of all bosses, he's still in a leadership position. His life will depend on how well he does. If he fucks up my product or my money, he dies, and I don't give a fuck whose pussy your dick is hypnotized by, that won't change." Standing, he reminded me, "Family is over everything. Don't let her make you forget that."

I was content with him agreeing to at least see how Carlos would do. From what he and Whiskee said, I had faith he'd excel in the role. If not, I'd done all that I could do.

Whiskee

L ate May

OF ALL THE HOMES, APARTMENTS, AND CONDOS
Beethoven and I had looked at in Rose Valley Hills, surprisingly, I was most in love with the penthouse suite at the
Rose Valley Hotel. Not only was it perfectly positioned on
the beach by the boardwalk, and close to the downtown and
art districts, but I loved how much smaller it was compared
to the homes I'd grown up in.

I loved how small and comfortable Mahogany's apartment was compared to my home. And the penthouse suite
was just as perfect. On top of the location, the convenience
of amenities the hotel offered were a luxury within themselves. Not only did they have a concierge service that took
care of shopping, deliveries, and setting up appointments,
but they also had two pools, a spa, a gym, and a dance studio
that I could see me and Mahogany having a time in, plus
two bars and a restaurant.

The main rooms of the suite had wall-to-wall windows that gave perfect views of the beach, and as I looked out into the rippling waves, I was in awe.

"This is it, baby," I told Beethoven, squeezing his hand. "This is what I want."

He placed a kiss to my neck. "Then this is what you'll get."

Releasing my hand, he walked over to the real estate agent to let her know this was what we wanted. Her name was Claudia, and she worked at *Wilson, Cane, Simpson, and Fisher.* She asked him if he wanted to make a cash offer or see about financing and Beethoven told her he'd pay cash. I don't think she was expecting a young Black man to offer to pay cash for a million-dollar penthouse suite, and I also didn't expect her to question how he obtained those funds.

She asked us to follow her back to the office to finalize some paperwork, and excitement bubbled over within me during the entire drive. I was leaving Memphis with the man I loved and my best friend. I would be able to have my own salon suite and do hair and makeup on a regular basis. Beethoven had decided to open dispensaries with Omari so I wouldn't have to worry about being with a man who was in the streets. The only thing that would have made life better was having my parents and my brother moving here with me.

Just thinking about that saddened me a little. Carlos said he was okay with me leaving and finally starting to do my own thing, but I still felt bad about it. That was why when we made it to Claudia's office, I hung back so I could call Carlos. With the transition of him going into production, he seemed to be more at peace. I hoped it would stay that way when the change was permanent, which would be after the wedding. Then, he would announce that Tim was taking Daddy's place, and Tim would appoint him as the head of production.

I called my brother, hoping he was free to answer. It took three rings, but eventually he answered with, "You good, sis?"

"I am. Are you?"

"Yeah, just running a few errands. I need to talk to you when you get back. It's something I've just been made aware of, and I want you to know too."

"Okay. Um... I just wanted to make sure you were really okay with me moving. With Mama and Daddy being gone... I don't want you to be alone."

He chuckled. "Sis, live your life. You've been a kept princess since you were born. It's time for you to get out the house, out the city, and do your own thing. Don't worry about me."

"I can't help but worry about you. You're my brother and I love you."

"I love you too. I won't lie and say I won't be lacking without my shadow, but this is for the best. Besides, I'll be heavy in the streets. You won't have to worry about me, lil stinky."

My eyes watered as I smiled. "Are you sure, Los?"

"I'm positive."

"Okay. If you change your mind, promise me you'll tell me."

"I promise."

"Okay, I'll talk to you when I get home."

"Aight."

After disconnecting the call, I headed for Claudia's office. I was surprised when, after a few minutes passed, I was informed it wouldn't just be Beethoven's name on the paperwork but mine too. I believed him when he said he wanted to have a true partnership, but this further confirmed it and increased my confidence in what we had.

The Next Morning

CARLOS WAS WAITING AT THE APARTMENT WHEN WE arrived, which meant he was serious about needing to talk to me. Beethoven grabbed my bag as he said, "I'll give y'all some privacy."

"This concerns you."

Setting our bags down, Beethoven sat next to me on the couch, while Carlos sat across from us in the recliner.

"Wassup?" Beethoven asked as I took his hand into mine.

"One of my pops trusted advisors came to me yesterday after our meeting. I mentioned there being some changes soon and he pulled me to the side to make sure that didn't include me stepping down and giving the business to your father."

"Why would he assume that?"

"Someone in your organization is talking. They're saying Tim is about to take over and that if I don't handle my business, he's going to kill me." Carlos sat up in his seat, forearms resting on his thighs. "But worse than that, they mentioned bugs that will soon lead to a raid. I'on know who it is, but y'all got a rat."

I was confused as to why this involved me. I was never included in conversations like this.

"What does this have to do with me?" I asked.

Carlos breathed deeply. "Your name has been swirling around too." His eyes shifted in Beethoven's direction. "Apparently, whoever the rat is knows who killed Mama and it's someone in his organization. They said we're dumb as fuck working with and sleeping with the family who put Mama in the grave."

The Glock Carlos rested on his thigh caused my heart to stop beating. My grip on Beethoven's hand loosened, but he didn't budge.

"Did you kill my mother?" Carlos asked. "And if it wasn't you, do you know who it was?"

Beethoven chuckled as he sat back on the couch. His level of calm only made me more anxious.

"When you pull a gun out, ain't shit else that needs to be said. It's in your best interest to use that mothafucka *now*."

"Wait, hold on." Lifting my hands, I stood between both seated men on wobbly legs. "We've made great progress. Le-let's not ruin that." I looked at Beethoven, and the confident smile on his face was the exact opposite of my brother's frown. Regardless of how dangerous and lethal Beethoven was, Carlos had never backed down from a challenge. If these two went at it, I honestly didn't know who would make it out alive.

"Los," I called, trying to get his eyes to focus on me instead of Beethoven. "If this person is a rat, can you even trust their information? It could be a false rumor."

"That's why I want him to tell me the truth."

"Baby," I called, voice shaky. "I know you didn't kill our mother... but do you know who did?"

His head bobbed once, and it felt like my entire world spun on its axis. I shared with him how much losing her

162

affected me to this day, and he knew who was responsible for her death?

"Before you start coming up with assumptions in your head, let me tell you the truth," he said, using my hand to sit me on his lap. Blocking Carlos out, he only focused on me. "The day I tried to get you the apartment and you shared with me the story of what happened to you and your mother, some of the details were familiar. I went to Pops about it, and he confirmed the robbery was done by someone in our organization."

He paused and took a deep breath. "In our family. I struggled with whether or not to tell you, but I handled it myself. The person who gave the order will be in a wheel-chair because of a bullet to his spine for the rest of his life. The shooter is still in a coma. He's not expected to wake up, and if he does, he's not expected to return to his normal life."

"What was the reason for the hit?" Carlos asked.

"They wanted to sit your father down. He wasn't there, so they went after his wife instead."

I didn't realize tears were streaming until Beethoven kissed them away. His grip around my waist tightened when he said, "I went against my own family to avenge yours." His eyes locked with Carlos's when he added, "That should prove I'm not letting anyone hurt her or come between us." Gently, he pushed me onto the couch next to him. "So if you gon' use that gun, you need to use it before I get to mine."

"I wish you would've told us this sooner," Carlos said.

"I didn't want to ruin things personally or professionally for something I took care of. If she mentioned wanting to know who was responsible for it, I would have told her then. But trust, they have been punished with a fate worse than death for what they did to Renee and the pain it left behind for both of you."

Carlos stood and I held my breath to see what he was going to do. I purposely shielded Beethoven's chest with my body, but again, he pushed me out of the way and stood. Slowly, Carlos's hand extended in his direction.

"Thank you. It ate at me and Pops to never know who was responsible. I 'preciate you giving us both some peace and for taking care of that."

"Thank you for letting me know about the rat. We knew about the bugs, but not that there was someone within our organization feeding out information. If they're talking to other families, there's no doubt in my mind they're talking to the feds too."

Since it seemed they were in a good space, I left. I wasn't exactly sure how I felt. I was glad the people responsible were punished, but this was the second thing Beethoven kept from me. Even with his reasoning behind it, that hurt. Was this something I'd have to accept to be with him—knowing he'd pick and choose what truths he shared and when to protect me?

A part of me was grateful for it because it kept me from stressing over things I didn't need to. The other part of me felt betrayed. Until I figured out which part meant the most, I'd keep the peace between me and Beethoven. The wedding was just a couple of weeks away, and I didn't need anything stopping that from happening. Not only was a huge amount of money at risk, but my brother's life was too.

Beethoven

T en Days Later

THINGS HAD BEEN... HEALTHY. NOT ALWAYS GOOD BUT healthy. A couple of days after the truth came out about Renee, Whiskee shut down on me. It was like she relived that night all over again and only Carlos could pull her out of it. I did share with him who the family members were, and after he was able to confirm their current states, it seemed to make him respect me more.

Whiskee expressed to me that she felt like she couldn't trust me because I kept important things from her. I made it clear to her that wasn't my intention, and that I thought I was protecting her. Because she was my woman, it was my responsibility to protect her in all ways—even ways she might not like. I wouldn't tell her something that would make her sad or stress her out if I didn't have to. But, to compromise, I promised to tell her need-to-know things even if I didn't like how it would make her feel.

When we came to that compromise, things became better than they ever had been between us.

Mama had been working with Mariam on the engagement party, which was tomorrow. Whiskee had been in Rose Valley Hills helping Mahogany find somewhere to stay when we all moved. And surprisingly, Carlos had been hanging out with me and the crew.

I was missing my wife, though, so I pulled up on her at the hotel in The Hills. When she opened the door and saw me standing behind it, she jumped into my arms. Three days had passed since she'd been in my arms, and I couldn't describe how good it felt to hold her.

"You're here," she cooed before kissing my neck.

"I missed you."

"I missed you too."

"I need to spend some time witchu, but I'ma leave tonight so you can stay with ya girl."

"Yay!"

After laughing and giving her a kiss, I told her to put on something casual and meet me downstairs at the bar. It only took a few minutes before she was walking down quickly with a smile. It made me feel good to know she missed me just as much as I missed her. I truly loved this woman, and it was crazy how deeply I cared for her in just over three months. It was crazy how a woman I was forced into marriage with had become the woman I truly wanted to spend the rest of my life with. In the beginning, I resented Pops and Carlos for putting us in this situation, but now, I was grateful.

"This has been perfect, baby. Thank you."

"Always. I'm glad you enjoyed yourself."

"I *always* enjoy myself with you. But this was my first time doing something so laid-back and romantic. I'll remember this forever."

"Lord knows you took enough pictures to."

Her giggle was like music to my ears as we walked through the hotel lobby. For our impromptu date, I took her on a gondola ride across the river. After that, we had dinner at the food hall and listened to some live music. As promised, I was about to return her to Mahogany so they could return to their girls' weekend. I hoped Mahogany was able to find her somewhere to live because I knew how important it was to them that we all move at the same time, which was also why I wanted to talk to my wife.

After we got onto the elevator I told her, "We will have to leave Memphis sooner than expected."

"Okay... but why?"

"Your pops' advisor was right. We do have a few rats and they've been working with the feds."

"What does that mean?"

"It means if we didn't find the rest of the bugs and anyone has been talking shit that suggests we're a criminal organization or alludes to any crimes committed, we're fucked. Good thing is, Pops has policies in place to keep himself, me, and our right hands and advisors from ever being personally attached to something like this, but if this is God's way of getting me out the way, I'm going to take it."

"Does he know about this?"

"Yeah. He knows. The feds have been watching for years, but this is the first time they've ever planted bugs. And if they have bugs planted..."

"They might have men planted too," she added.

I nodded. "Exactly."

"Okay, so we'll leave right after the wedding. After Los is named the head of production."

Sighing, I ran my hand down my neck. "That's the plan."

She turned toward me as the elevator dinged on their floor. "You don't sound like your confident self."

"I'm not concerned about something happening to your brother. I'll talk to him and recommend he decline the position, but that's on him. If he wants to stay and hope the RICO charges won't come, or at least not affect him, that's on him."

"Then what are you concerned about?" she asked, holding my hand as we walked down the hall.

"How Pops is going to react to me leaving. Family is everything to him. He's going to see me leaving as betrayal."

"But this has been your plan for a while. It's just a coincidence that this is happening at the same time."

"You and I know that, but he won't care. So I'm hoping the raids won't happen any time soon. I need to get you out the city and get us settled here before anything else happens with the business."

She released a hard breath as her expression turned serious. This was why I didn't want to talk to her about things like this, but I promised I'd keep her in the loop.

"We're going to be aight, bae. Okay?"

Her eyes found mine as she nodded. "Okay." When her arms wrapped around my neck, she held me longer than she ever had before. The risk of prison was always on the table when you lived this lifestyle. I never cared until now. Not until I had someone to lose...

Whiskee

B efore The Engagement Party

THE NEWS BEETHOVEN SHARED WITH ME YESTERDAY weighed on me heavily. I hoped I would be able to convince Carlos to get out before anything happened, but I didn't think he would. Still, I wanted to talk to him about it, and I was glad Lisa offered to have a dinner for just a few of our closest friends and some of Beethoven's family from her side before the actual engagement party tonight.

We decided to do the party three days before the wedding since it was planned so quickly. What I wasn't expecting was to have to move immediately after, but I was excited about it and willing to do just about anything to get my happily ever after.

I wasn't looking forward to being around Tim or the Smith family, but the engagement party was for their benefit. They needed to believe that, despite how quickly things progressed between Beethoven and I, that our love was real.

That way, they'd not only accept my father's men and allow Tim to remain our supplier, but also accept my brother as the head of production.

Even with the constant prayers I was sending up that Carlos would reject the position, my gut was telling me he wouldn't. This lifestyle was all he knew. He expected it to end badly, unfortunately, after what happened to our father. It broke my heart knowing my brother was so dedicated to something so deadly, but it was his choice and I had to accept it.

"Girrrl, your mama-in-law did her big one with this dinner," Mahogany said, wrapping her arm around mine.

There was no denying that. Not only did she have Graceland Pierce as the planner along with Mariam, but she also hired the best private chef in Memphis for the engagement party and had Antonne and Haley prepare a savory and sweet grazing table feast with paired wine and whisky options for tonight. The décor was beautiful. The white and gold color scheme made me feel like royalty. Arranged marriage or not, I was truly happy in this moment.

"I know, right? I wasn't expecting Lisa to do all this, but she's such a sweetheart. She said she wanted this to be special for us, no matter what brought us together. I really love that lady. I couldn't have asked for a better mother-in-law."

"Excuse me, bae," Beethoven said, gently gripping my wrist. "Can I steal you away for a second?"

"Um... sure. What are you up to?"

"You'll see."

He led me over to the balloon and bouquet arch. Lisa's smile was wide as she and Keith, her man, pulled a large sheet down that revealed a picture of Mama and Robert

Carter on their wedding day. I thought my heart would stop and never work again. Tears blurred my eyes, and my knees grew weak as I stared at the picture. Beethoven placed a kiss to my cheek and caught a few tears, giving me time to process the visual before me.

Once I was composed, Carlos and Mahogany made their way behind me as Beethoven kneeled in front of me.

Even though we were already engaged to be married, I was still completely caught off guard by his gesture as I watched him pull a beautiful pear-shaped diamond out of his pocket.

"When we first agreed to this, it was by force. Now, it's by choice." Beethoven kissed my shaking hand. "Whiskee Shiann Carter, will you marry me?"

Nodding, I wiggled my fingers in his face, causing him to laugh as he slipped the gorgeous rock onto my ring finger. He stood as those around us clapped, pulling me into his warm embrace.

"I love you, bae," he whispered against my lips before kissing them.

"Mm... I love you too," I replied, wrapping my hands around his neck as I returned his kisses.

The sound of the doorbell ringing wasn't enough to pull me away. I didn't release his lips until I heard Keith say, "Were they expecting you?"

Beethoven and I turned toward the entry way at the same time, and anger immediately began to fill me at the sight of Tim.

This was supposed to be an intimate moment of peace. One that would allow us to celebrate our love purely with those we trusted most and it not be about business. I had accepted dealing with Tim at the engagement party... not here. Beethoven gave my hand a gentle squeeze as Carlos made his way to the other side of me.

"Who told you about this?" Beethoven asked.

"Omari."

All eyes were on Omari as he headed in Tim's direction.

"You knew how important this dinner was to us, cuz," Beethoven said. "Why would you tell him to come here?"

"Because regardless of your disloyalty, I'ma *always* look out for Unc. Family is over everything, and hooking up with the Carters has made you forget that."

Beethoven pushed me toward my brother as his father stepped into his personal space.

"Did you think I wouldn't find out what you had planned? That you were going to leave the city and act like I haven't made you the man you are today? You think I'm gon' let you go legit and leave me?"

"It doesn't matter what you think you're going to let me do. I'm a grown ass man, and there's nothing you can do to stop me."

Both men were like lightning when they pulled their guns. While Beethoven's was aimed at his father, Tim's was aimed at me.

"I can kill them both with one bullet," Tim taunted as Omari pulled his weapon, aiming it at Beethoven, and I saw the moment my husband's heart broke. Omari hadn't been just his right-hand man; he was his closest cousin. If Beethoven made it clear that he trusted anyone—it was Omari.

"You can try, and you'll be dead before the bullet even makes contact," Beethoven replied, forcing Tim to look at him.

"You'd kill me over a bitch, son? That's where we at with it now?"

Beethoven chuckled as his head shook. He took a step in his father's direction. The slight distraction allowed Carlos to pull me behind him. I closed my eyes and pulled in a deep breath, taking Mahogany's hand into mine. It made me proud to see my brother standing by my man, but Lord knows I hated it had to even come to this.

"Where we at with it... is that's my wife and my brother. You gave them to me, and I will protect them and my chance at a new life and freedom at all costs." He took another step in his father's direction. "Don't make me choose between you and her, Pops." A slow smile spread his lips as his head tilted. "You're going to lose."

As I continued to pray, it seemed like time froze. One second, I was sure Tim and Omari were about to stand down. Their guns lowered and they turned to leave. The next, Tim was looking back at us with an evil glare that shook me to my core. His arm lifted, but the bullet meant for me went into my brother as he fired.

I wasn't sure whose bullets hit Tim and Omari as he and Beethoven unloaded their clips. All I knew was, my brother's body leaked as he lay on top of me... and if I lost him... God may as well take me tonight too.

"You're so stubborn it's ridiculous," I nagged, angry that Carlos refused to stay in the hospital overnight for observation. Thankfully, the bullet went straight through his side. No major damage was done, and he hadn't lost a significant amount of blood.

Both Tim and Omari were killed, and I wasn't sure how I felt about that. I was glad they hadn't been able to hurt anyone else, but I was hurt over Beethoven's father and cousin being dead. I didn't know how he was handling the losses because he hadn't been at the hospital. He wanted to be, but there were too many loose ends for him to tie up at his mom's place to babysit me.

"They wrapped me up and gave me some prescriptions, so I'm good," Carlos said, arm tossed over my shoulder as I helped him get into bed.

"Still, you should have stayed in the hospital like they advised, Carlos."

Sucking his teeth, he grimaced as he tried to get comfortable in bed. "This won't be the first time you've had to change the dressing over a gunshot wound. I'll be good."

There was no point in me going back and forth with him, so I put his phone within his reach and told him I'd be in the room next door if he needed me. I was in the process of returning calls and replying to text messages when Beethoven called and told me he was outside. My heart dropped into the pit of my stomach. There was no point in avoiding him or this conversation. If he felt some type of way about his family being gone, it was better we handle the situation now instead of later. I would understand if he no longer wanted to be with me, but I hoped that wouldn't be the case.

It felt like it took me forever to get to the front door, but when I did, Beethoven wasted no time pulling me into his arms. For a moment, I was so in shock I couldn't hug him back. When I realized he was happy to see me, I hugged him back. We stood there for a while in a much-needed embrace before going into the sitting room.

"I won't ask if you're okay," I said, "Is there... anything I can do?"

His head shook as he squeezed my thigh and stared into the distance. "Nah."

"I know this has to be a lot for you. Omari betraying you and your dad…"

Beethoven's head hung. His Adam's apple bobbed as he swallowed hard.

"My pops was going to kill you." Scoffing, Beethoven shook his head. "I don't know if it was my bullets or your brother's but…"

"I'm so sorry, baby." Scooting closer, I wrapped my arms around him. "I'm sorry it had to come to this. I would have never asked you to choose."

"You wouldn't have had to." His eyes found mine. "When it comes to you, it's never a choice. Do I wish he and my cousin were alive? Hell fuckin' yeah. But when them guns start firing, nothing matters but staying alive. He chose to shoot, and he suffered the consequence. It's as simple as that."

"It's not as simple as that, Bay. That was your father. Regardless of how his actions had you questioning his character lately, that was your father. I know what it feels like to lose one. You can play tough with everyone else, but you don't have to do that with me."

His leg started to shake, and I prepared for what I knew was about to come. It took a while, but eventually his head shook as tears started to flow.

"Why would he do that shit, Whiskee?" he asked, and the sight of his tears made my own threaten to fall. "He *knew* I would kill him. Why would he try me like that?"

I had no answer for him, and as his sobs grew louder, it didn't seem to matter. I did the only thing I knew to do— hold him and allow him to release everything he'd been holding inside while I prayed.

Beethoven

F ifteen Months Later

LIFE WAS GOOD.

It took a hell of a lot of prayer, therapy, love, and healing to get here... but life was good.

After the shooting, I shut down. I didn't regret protecting Whiskee and Carlos, but I hated that my father and cousin had to die because of it. It didn't matter how much my family or therapist told me it was their choice to betray me and shoot first, that didn't fully remove the guilt, pain, and anger that consumed me. Even now, I had my days where I couldn't get over that emotional hill, but I'd learned to take it one day at a time.

Me and Whiskee made the move to Rose Valley Hills, and so did Mahogany and Carlos. Carlos was, in fact, damn good at creating strains and distribution. Together, we'd created a dispensary here in Rose Valley Hills that had been open for three months and was doing exceptionally well. We had plans of opening dispensaries all over the country, but for now, we were content with the success of our first store.

Whiskee had opened her own salon suites business. She did hair and makeup as well, but with the suites, the bulk of her profit came from other stylists that were renting space.

Mahogany was still doing her thing as an influencer and brand ambassador. At the moment, she was on some island to potentially sign her first six-figure brand contract.

Mama and Keith had finally gotten married. I wasn't sure if it was Pops' death or the shooting showing them the importance of life, but I was glad she'd finally said yes.

The Carter and Smith organizations had still combined in Memphis, but under their new leadership, they were raided and shut down about two months after we left the city. A part of me was glad Pops and Robert weren't around to see the demise of the empires they'd devoted their lives to building.

All in all...

Life was good.

The only thing that was going to make it better was the birth of my son.

Whiskee and I eloped in Vegas the day before Valentine's Day. After everything that happened, we decided to keep our exchanging of vows sacred and private. We did, however, have a party with our family and friends to celebrate when we got back home. Our son was conceived on our honeymoon, and I couldn't wait for him to enter our little world.

This life was slower and more peaceful than the one I'd been accustomed to. I missed my cousin and my father, but my life had new purpose and a different meaning now. The crew back home came to visit often, and I was glad my son would be able to grow up with their kids, even though he'd be a little younger than them.

The sound of Whiskee and Mahogany's laughter made me smile like it always did as they wrapped up their Face-Time call. If nothing else, I could count on them to be somewhere giggling and enjoying each other like nothing else mattered. As I entered our bedroom, my wife's smile widened at the sight of me. I didn't know how it was possible, but it seemed like our love grew day by day.

"You ready to go?" I asked, walking over to the bed.

"Not yet. Come lay with me first."

I climbed into bed behind her and wrapped her up in my arms. We were about to head to Memphis for Mama's birthday, and we'd also use the trip to connect with some friends. It would be the last trip we took until after Whiskee gave birth. I rubbed her stomach, and it didn't take long for Winston to start moving around.

"I was thinking while we're in town we can go back to that supper club where we had our first date," Whiskee suggested. "I won't be able to drink, but you can. And we can dance until my feet hurt."

Her giggle made me smile as I placed kisses on her neck. "We can do that, and I won't need any alcohol. You're the strongest, sweetest, smoothest Whiskee I'll ever need."

Turning in my arms, Whiskee wrapped her arm around my neck and kissed me. I never thought things would turn out this way, but I would never complain. I was grateful to God for my wife and son, for the peace that had consumed my life, and for the people in it whom I knew truly meant me well.

The End

Karrington is up next, but his book will be in the Mister series, not the Protector series.

Also by B. Love

Afterword

Let's connect!

Mailing list - https://bit.ly/MLBLove22
On all social media - @authorblove
If you rave about this book on TikTok, tag me, and let's make a duet!
For exclusive eBooks, paperbacks, and audiobooks –
www.prolificpenpusher.net

We hate errors, but we are human! If the B. Love team leaves any grammatical errors behind, do us a kindness and send them to us directly in an email to emailblove@gmail.com with ERRORS as the subject line.
As always, if you enjoyed this book, please leave a review on Amazon/Goodreads, recommend it on social media and/or to a friend, and mark it as READ on your Goodreads profile.

Follow B. on Amazon for updates on her releases by clicking <u>here</u>.

By the Book with B. Podcast – bit.ly/ bythebookwithb

Made in the USA
Columbia, SC
25 June 2024

37530921R00102